"Of course, you'll be going out this evening."

Serena's voice was composed as they walked out to the street again. And to his sharp "Why do you say that?", she went on, "Well, you wouldn't want to waste your evening."

"Are you saying that I'm wasting my day?" His voice had an edge to it.

"Good heavens, no, that would be ill-mannered of me. I'm having a lovely day, but if I were you, I don't think I'd want to take me out."

"Why not, Serena?" His voice was silky.

"Well, for one thing, you've seen all this before, haven't you? And I'm not witty or fascinating or amusing, and I'm nothing much to look at."

"What an abominable girl you are!" he said, stopping abruptly and turning her to face him.

Betty Neels is well-known for her romances set in the Netherlands, which is hardly surprising. She married a Dutchman and spent the first twelve years of their marriage living in Holland and working as a nurse. Today, she and her husband make their home in an ancient stone cottage in England's West Country, but they return to Holland often. She loves to explore tiny villages and tour privately owned homes there, in order to lend an air of authenticity to the background of her books.

Books by Betty Neels

HARLEQUIN ROMANCE
3053—THE CHAIN OF DESTINY
3071—HILLTOP TRYST
3084—THE CONVENIENT WIFE
3105—THE GIRL WITH GREEN EYES
3131—A SUITABLE MATCH
3149—ROSES HAVE THORNS

A LITTLE MOONLIGHT

Betty Neels

Harlequin Books

TORONTO • NEW YORK • LONDON
AMSTERDAM • PARIS • SYDNEY • HAMBURG
STOCKHOLM • ATHENS • TOKYO • MILAN

Original hardcover edition published in 1991
by Mills & Boon Limited

ISBN 0-373-03161-0

Harlequin Romance first edition November 1991

A LITTLE MOONLIGHT

CHAPTER ONE

It was mid-September and the day had been grey so that dusk had come early. Almost every window in the Royal Hospital was lighted, making a cheerful splash of colour amid the dingy streets of small houses and corner shops over which it towered. Only on the top floor of the hospital, where the windows were much smaller, were they in darkness—all save one, a corner room, furnished in a businesslike way with filing cabinets, shelves of reference books, a large desk on which was an electric typewriter, a computer and a word-processor, a small hard chair against one wall and another more comfortable one behind the desk.

There was a girl sitting in it, a smallish person with a tidy head of mousy hair pinned severely into a bun, and an ordinary face whose small beaky nose and wide mouth were enlivened by large hazel eyes, fringed with a long set of curling lashes. She was typing with the ease of long practice, frowning over the sheet of handwriting beside her, but presently she stopped. The writing was by no means easy to read and she was used to that, but she had come to a halt. After a minute's frustrated study she spoke her mind to the empty room.

'Well, now what? Is it endometrioma or endometriosis? Why must he use such long words, and why wasn't he taught to write properly?' She sounded vexed, and for a good reason; it was long after five o'clock, the top floor, used by typists and clerks and administration staff, had become empty and quiet and she was lonely, hungry and getting rapidly more annoyed. 'It's all very well for him,' she went on, talking out loud to keep her spirits up, 'he'll be home, with his feet up, while his wife gets his supper...'

'Actually,' said a deep slow voice from behind her, 'he's here, although the picture you paint of domestic bliss is tempting.'

The girl shot round in her chair, but before she could speak the man standing in the doorway went on, 'I feel that I should apologise for my writing—it is, I'm afraid, too late to do much about that, and as for the long words, they are inevitable in our profession.' He advanced into the room and stood looking down at her. 'Why have I not seen you before now, and where is Miss Payne?'

She looked up at him with a touch of impatience, untroubled by the awe he engendered in the regular hospital staff. 'Miss Payne is off sick—influenza.' She cast an eye over the small pile of work still to be done. 'And probably overwork, from the look of these.'

'Your name?' he asked with cold courtesy.

'Serena Proudfoot.' Her arched silky eyebrows asked the question she didn't utter.

'Dr ter Feulen.'

'Oh, I've heard about you, you're a Dutch baron as well...' She smiled at him with the air of one ready to forgive him for that.

He was a handsome man, with grizzled hair and pale blue eyes as cold as a winter sea; moreover, he was a splendid height and broad-shouldered. Serena had only half believed the other girls who worked in administration and dealt with the medical correspondence when they had enthused about Dr ter Feulen, but she could see that they had been right. All the same, he appeared to be both arrogant and sarcastic. He ignored the remark and she stopped smiling.

'You are from an agency?' he queried.

'Yes, just as a temporary until Miss Payne is well again. And now, if you don't mind, I'll get on...'

He didn't move. 'Why are you working late?'

A silly question, but she answered it patiently. 'Because there was a backlog of your letters to be done and I was warned that you would expect them ready for your signature before you left the hospital.'

'And are they ready?'

'No, but if I can be left in peace to type them you can have them in half an hour.'

He laughed suddenly. 'Have you been working long as a typist?'

'Several years.'

'But never in a hospital, that is obvious.' He strolled back to the door. 'Be good enough to bring them to the consultants' room when you are ready, please. Perhaps no one told you that we don't watch the clock in hospital. It is to be hoped that Miss Payne is soon back at her desk.'

He had gone before Serena could utter her heartfelt agreement.

She put a fresh sheet of paper into her machine. 'And why did he have to come here in the first place?' she demanded of the empty room.

'Why, to see what had happened to my letters,' observed Dr ter Feulen. He had returned and was standing in the doorway again. 'I have come back to warn you that I have an outpatients' clinic in the morning and you will have a good deal of work to do in consequence. So let us have no more grumbling about late hours; Miss Payne never uttered a word.'

'More fool her,' said Serena with spirit. She answered his goodnight with cold asperity.

It was almost an hour later when she covered her machine and turned out the lights. The consultants' room was on the ground floor. She tapped on the door and, since no one answered, opened it and went in. There was only one small table light on and the large, gloomy room was dim. She laid the papers she had been typing on the ponderous centre table and turned to go again. A faint sound stopped her; Dr ter Feulen, his vast person stretched at ease in a leather armchair, his large feet, shod in the finest shoe leather, resting on a nearby coffee-table, was asleep and, without any loss of dignity, snoring gently. She stood and looked at him. He really was extremely good-looking, although now that she was able to study his face at her leisure, she could see that he was very tired.

She was tired too. She made her way from the room and out of the hospital and joined the queue at the nearest bus-stop.

She got off the bus at East Sheen and walked down a side street leading to a road lined with a terrace of red brick Edwardian villas, all very well kept. Halfway down she took out a key and let herself into the house through its pristine black-painted door, hung her coat in the narrow hall and went into the sitting-room. Her mother was there, sitting before a gas fire reading. She looked up as Serena went in.

'You're late.' She glanced reproachfully at the clock on the mantelpiece. 'I just didn't feel like getting the supper.' She smiled charmingly at her daughter. 'Aren't I a lazy old mother? It's cottage pie and you make such a good one, and if the oven's on I thought you might make one of your fruit tarts.'

Serena crossed the rather shabby room and kissed her mother. 'I'll go and start the pie,' was all she said. 'I'm sorry if you've had a bad day.'

'My nerves,' said Mrs Proudfoot, 'and all the worry of managing on the pension... If only your father had known...'

'We manage quite well,' replied Serena matter-of-factly. 'The pension isn't so bad, Mother, and there's my money.'

'Oh, I do know, darling, but you have no idea how unhappy I am when I think of all the things you're missing... dances and theatres and trips abroad. You might have been married by now—you're twenty-five...'

Mrs Proudfoot eyed her daughter with a look of resignation; how she had come to have this serious, rather plain girl who made no push to get herself a husband was something she couldn't understand. She had been considered quite pretty as a girl, and even now in her fifties she was still that, or so she told herself. That a good deal of the pension went on cosmetics and hairdressers and pretty clothes was something she never dwelt on. Serena had an allowance from her salary—not a big one, it was true, but then at her age she didn't need expensive creams and lotions, and since she worked in some dreary office for five days out of the seven, she didn't need many clothes. Mrs Proudfoot, a good-natured woman as long as she had her own way, said kindly, 'I saw such a pretty blouse today, just right for you, darling, it would cheer up your skirts.' She picked up her book. 'I won't keep you gossiping, or we'll never get supper.'

Serena went into the kitchen, peeled potatoes for the cottage pie, minced yesterday's joint and, while the potatoes cooked, made pastry for the tart. She was tired, too tired to summon the energy to point out to her mother that she had had a long and exhausting day and a slow bus ride home, standing all the way. Besides, she loved her mother and quite understood that after years of being spoilt by her husband, she was quite unable to alter her way of life.

She made her pastry and thought about Dr ter Feulen. A very ill-tempered man, she reflected, possibly overworked, but there had been no need for him to have been quite so rude. He had looked very tired, sleeping in his chair. She wondered what his home life was like. With no wife he probably lived in a service flat and cooked lonely meals for himself, and that was why he had been so terse. She put the tart in the oven with the pie and went across the hall to set the table for their supper. It made a lot of extra work, fetching the cloth and napkins and cutlery and the crystal glasses her mother insisted on using, but as she had pointed out many times, standards had to be kept up at all costs. Serena, who ate a hasty breakfast in the small kitchen before she left for work, would have been quite happy to have eaten her supper there too.

They ate their supper presently while Mrs Proudfoot reminisced gently about earlier days. 'We had old Sadie then,' she reminded Serena. 'Such a pity she decided to retire, she kept the house so well—if only my health were better!' She sighed, and Serena asked sympathetically,

'Have you had a bad day, Mother?'

'My dear child, I seldom have a good one. Just the effort to go shopping and get myself a morsel to eat during the day exhausts me.' Mrs Proudfoot contrived to look as though she were bravely combating ill health without complaint. 'I'll have a morsel more of that pie, darling, I've eaten almost nothing all day.'

It was hard to believe. She was plump and still pretty in her fifties, dressed with taste and at some expense and not lacking the attention of the hairdresser and the beauty salon, both of which took up a good deal of her empty days. While her husband had been alive there had been a nanny for Serena and someone to run the house, and as she was good-naturedly indolent by nature, it had never entered her head to alter her way of living. From time to time she deplored the fact that Serena had inherited none of her good looks, but it hadn't entered her head to do anything about it. Serena had uncomplainingly taken a course of shorthand and typing and found herself a job so that there was enough money for her mother to continue to live more or less as she had always done. If, now and again, she wished for something more from life than she was getting, she stifled the thought.

'I shall be late home tomorrow too,' she told her mother. 'This doctor whose work I'm doing warned me this evening.'

Mrs Proudfoot dismissed him with a wave of the hand. 'How perfectly horrid of him! You should have told him that you're needed at home in the evenings—that you have a mother in poor health.'

'Yes—well, if I did, Mother, he would probably tell someone to get another typist until his usual one gets back from sick leave. The next job might be even more awkward . . .'

Mrs Proudfoot sighed. 'Ah, well, I suppose I must manage. Perhaps I'll go to that little restaurant in Albert Street and have a light meal.' She added hastily, 'You could make yourself an omelette when you get in?'

Serena said, without rancour, 'Yes, Mother,' and went to fetch the coffee.

The following morning passed very much as usual—letters and reports and accounts. Judging by the number of the latter, Serena guessed that Dr ter Feulen had a large practice. While she typed she mused; a doctor's life would never be dull; anti-social hours, short nights perhaps, interrupted meals and tiresome patients. Very hard on their wives... She paused to think about that, but they wouldn't be dull either, because no two days would be the same, unlike her own days which were, to say the least, monotonous.

She went to the canteen for her coffee with two of the other medical typists and then, mindful of Dr ter Feulen's warning, went back to her desk. There were still a few odds and ends to clear up and she wanted to be ready for the mass of work he had predicted.

She had been sitting for perhaps five minutes, her desk tidied, her hands poised over the first short report, when the phone at the other end of the room rang.

Mrs Dunn, the senior and the least hard-working of the typists, picked it up, listened and put it down again. 'Miss Proudfoot, you're to go to OPD, and take your notebook with you. And look sharp, Dr ter Feulen doesn't like to be kept waiting.'

Serena finished the report, laid it neatly on her desk, took her time getting notebook and pencil and got up without haste.

'Do hurry, Miss Proudfoot!' hissed Mrs Dunn. 'Dr ter Feulen mustn't be kept waiting; I've told you that already.'

'Yes, Mrs Dunn.' Serena, still without haste, began the tortuous journey through the hospital to the Out-patient Department. Dr ter Feulen had had ample time to warn her that she would be wanted in OPD, and if he thought she would come running the moment he wanted her, he must think again!

He was in his consulting-room, looking at X-rays with his registrar, and Serena paused inside the door to ask, 'You sent for me, sir?'

He looked over his shoulder. 'Ah, Miss Proudfoot, you will be good enough to take notes of the patients, together with their names and case sheet numbers, get them typed out and let me have them this evening.'

'If I can get them finished by then,' observed Serena matter-of-factly. 'It depends on how many patients there are, doesn't it?'

'In that case it will be necessary for you to remain until you have finished, will it not?' He raised thick eyebrows. 'I believe I warned you that you might have to work late today.'

'So you did,' said Serena cheerfully. 'Is this where I'm to work?'

The eyebrows stayed up, and judging by the look on the registrar's face she wasn't behaving as Miss Payne would have done. 'Yes, this is the place. Be good enough to sit on that chair over there. If you are uncertain about anything you are to say so at once. I doubt if you have the same high standards of medical knowledge as Miss Payne has.'

'Well, no, I don't suppose I have, but then she's been at it for twenty years, hasn't she?' She gave him a friendly smile. 'I dare say I'll be as good in twenty years' time.'

Outpatients Sister came in then and Serena settled on to her hard chair, pencil poised, looking efficient, while her thoughts wandered. It seemed to her that Dr ter Feulen was a crusty bachelor, much in need of a wife and children to bring out the softer side of his nature; he must have one buried away somewhere under that bitingly cold manner.

Surprisingly it came to light during the morning's session. It was a different man sitting at the desk now, listening patiently to his patients, women of all ages, reassuring them that they hadn't got cancer, examining them at length and laying before them the treatments they needed.

Serena's pencil flew over the pages, occasionally faltering at some long-winded word which escaped her knowledge. All the same, when Dr ter Feulen asked her between patients, 'You are getting all this down, Miss Proudfoot?' she said composedly,

'Yes, thank you, sir.'

When the clinic was over she would ask the registrar about the words she hadn't managed to get down.

It was almost two o'clock when the last patient went away and Sister and one of the nurses started clearing up. Dr ter Feulen and his registrar got to their feet and started for the door. Serena stayed where she was, praying silently that they would part company, so that she could get the registrar on his own, but instead of that Dr ter Feulen paused in the doorway, then walked back to her.

'Well, what didn't you get down?'

It annoyed her that he took it for granted that she hadn't been able to cope. She reeled off several words she had been unable to spell and added with some spirit, 'I've done my best, sir, but please remember that I'm not Miss Payne.'

She saw the registrar's face out of the corner of her eye. Shocked horror were the only words to describe it, and then she heard Sister's hissed breath. It struck her that she wasn't at all suitable to work for a leading consultant in a famous teaching hospital. She didn't stand in suitable awe of him, so it was perhaps a good thing that Miss Payne would be back shortly and she could return to her typing agency and be given a job in a warehouse or a factory, typing invoices against a background of uninhibited voices.

'The words?' asked Dr ter Feulen. 'Kindly repeat them.'

She did, and with a brief nod he went away, leaving her to gather up her notebook and pencil and go to the canteen. Midday dinner was long over. She had some soup and a roll and a pot of tea, and then hurried back to her desk. She had enough work to keep her busy until the evening.

She hadn't finished when the other typists went home at half-past five. A nearby church clock had struck six when the phone rang. 'Bring your work down to the consultants' room when it is finished, Miss Proudfoot.'

He hung up before she could so much as breathe a 'yes, sir'.

Half an hour later, dressed in her outdoor things, she knocked on the door and was bidden to enter. He was sitting at the table, writing, but rather to her surprise he got up as she went in.

'Ah, thank you, Miss Proudfoot.' He glanced at his watch. 'I trust your evening has not been spoiled.'

Serena assured him that it hadn't. 'I hardly ever go out in the evening,' she told him chattily, disposed to be friendly since he was still working himself. Speaking her thought out loud, she added, 'Well, you're not as tired as you were last night—you were asleep, you know, and snoring just a little. Had you had a busy day?'

He regarded her with some surprise. 'Yes, I had. Tell me, Miss Proudfoot, do you take an interest in everyone you meet?'

'Well, yes, most people.' She saw him frown. 'You think I'm being nosy and I suppose I ought to treat you with respect—you are a senior consultant. I must try and remember that while I'm here.'

'It might be as well! Goodnight, Miss Proudfoot, and thank you.'

'Goodnight, sir. I should go home and have an early night if you can—you look tired, almost as tired as you did yesterday.'

She closed the door quietly as she went out and forgot him while she racked her brains for a suitable meal to cook when she got home; something quick, but it would have to be tempting because of her mother's poor appetite...

Dr ter Feulen resumed his seat but made no attempt to continue his writing. He sat looking at nothing in particular, and presently he smiled.

Mrs Proudfoot was out of sorts when Serena got home. 'Really, darling,' she began as soon as Serena put her head round the sitting-room door, 'this is too bad; I've been alone all day!'

Serena kissed her mother's cheek. 'You went out for a meal?'

'Well, yes, but that's not the point. I'm really not well enough to be left alone for hours on end.' Her mother's pretty face puckered like a child's and Serena made haste to say,

'Well, as far as I know, I'll be home on time tomorrow, and the day after is Saturday.'

Her mother brightened. 'Ah, yes, I've asked one or two people in for the evening, so we might have a rubber or two of bridge. If you'd make some of those dear little savoury biscuits we could have coffee...'

'Yes, of course, and now how about an omelette? And could we eat it in the kitchen? It's a bit late and I've had quite a busy day.'

Mrs Proudfoot sighed. 'Well, just this once, although I do deplore this slovenly way of eating in the kitchen.'

Saturday morning was always set aside for shopping. Mrs Proudfoot liked to go into Richmond and have coffee at one or other of the smart cafés, and then after a leisurely stroll around the boutiques and dress shops she would visit an art gallery or have more coffee with acquaintances while Serena did the household shopping.

Serena, a laden basket on one arm, examining cauliflowers at the greengrocer's, failed to see Dr ter Feulen, driving his Bentley Turbo RLWB down the busy street. But he saw her, and although he didn't slacken speed he had ample time to note the shopping basket.

Three people came in that evening to play bridge, Mrs Pratt from the residential hotel near the river, Mr Twill who owned an antique shop in Richmond and Mr King, a retired civil servant who had spent a good deal of his life in foreign parts and never tired of talking of them. The four of them settled down to play, and Serena busied herself with drinks and presently went away to make coffee and arrange the savoury biscuits and some sandwiches on plates. It had never been suggested that she should play, and, since she was hopeless at the game, she accepted this as reasonable, and if sometimes she wished that her Saturday evenings were a little more entertaining she never voiced the thought.

Presently she settled down in a chair by the window, ready with a polite reply if any of the players spoke to her while she knitted a mohair cardigan for her mother; the fine wool made her sneeze and covered everything in fairylike threads. While she knitted she allowed her thoughts to stray. Since her teens she had known that she had no looks to speak of, and that had made her shy with people of her own age. Moreover, she had never mastered the airy, amusing chatter which her friends seemed to have acquired without any effort. She had friends, but somehow the pleasant social life they enjoyed had passed her by, largely because her mother had so often hindered her from taking part in it—never with obvious intention, but the sight of her mother with a woebegone face, pleading with her not to take any notice of the migraine which she was suffering, but to go out and enjoy herself; or a sad face bravely smiling at the prospect of a lonely evening, had had their effect over the years. Serena stayed at home or, if her mother went to a cinema or theatre, went with her. That couldn't stop her dreaming—impossible dreams, she was the first to admit, in which some handsome man would meet her and fall instantly in love and marry her. He would have a charming home and money enough so that if she wanted new clothes—fashionable ones, not the sober, hard-wearing ones she bought now—she could walk into a boutique and indulge her choice, and there would be children, nice cuddly babies, and someone to help in the house.

She was aroused from these pleasant thoughts by her mother's voice. 'Darling, we would all love some more coffee and some more of those dear little sandwiches you make so nicely.'

The evening ended, Serena tidied up, saw her mother to bed and went to her own room. It was a lovely night. Ready for bed, swathed in her dressing-gown, she opened her window wide and looked up at the sky. It was bright with stars and the light of the enormous moon creeping slowly above the housetops.

She addressed the moon softly. 'It's funny to think that you're shining down on all kinds of people. It would be nice to know who else is looking at you this very minute.'

Dr ter Feulen was one of them, pausing to look up as he strode across the hospital courtyard to his car after the emergency operation he had just performed and which had made havoc of his evening. He was tired, and for no reason at all he remembered the neat, plain girl with the lovely eyes who had bidden him have an early night. She would be in bed long ago, he reflected; it was easy to imagine the staid well-ordered life she led. A little moonlight might do her a great deal of good. He laughed at the thought, got into the car and drove himself home.

*   *   *

It was towards the end of the following week that Serena, once more working late, had another visit from Dr ter Feulen. He came without warning, and she stopped typing and sat, her hands in her lap, waiting for what she felt sure was coming. The excellent Miss Payne would be returning and she would no longer be needed. She was surprised how the thought depressed her, for she hadn't found the work easy at the hospital. Dr ter Feulen was hardly the easiest of taskmasters; in fact he was impatient, frequently ill-tempered and a perfectionist who expected everyone else to be perfect. She watched him cross the room towards her and wondered why he should be the one to tell her and not Mrs Dunn. After all, he had nothing to do with engaging the administrative staff, permanent or otherwise.

Dr ter Feulen drew up a chair and sat down opposite to her, wishing her an austere good evening as he did so.

'Good evening, sir,' said Serena, and added in a businesslike voice, 'I haven't finished your letters. Do you want me to take them anywhere for you to sign?' She glanced at the clock and added tartly, 'I'll be another fifteen minutes, provided I'm not interrupted.'

'I am interrupting you, but for a good reason, Miss Proudfoot. I have been to see Miss Payne. She has decided to retire and I have come to offer you her job.'

Serena stared at him, her eyes round with amazement. 'Me? Do Miss Payne's work? I couldn't possibly! She never uttered a word, you said, and I grumble—besides, you don't...' She paused and went a rather pretty pink.

'Like you?' He studied her face, alight with surprise and near-panic, and reflected that a few similar shocks would do much to improve her looks. 'Liking has very little to do with it. Let me tell you something, Miss Proudfoot. Miss Payne, as you so succinctly put it, never uttered a word at her awkward hours, but she wasn't afraid of me. You aren't afraid of me either, are you?'

She thought about it. 'No, I don't think I am.'

'Good. Then that's settled. You don't need to see anyone about it, I'll attend to the details. You will be better paid, of course.' He got up from his chair. 'Oh, and I shall be returning to Holland in two weeks' time. I have a series of lectures to give and as I'm a consultant at several hospitals there I shall be operating for several weeks. I am also writing a book. I shall want you with me, of course.'

Serena was speechless, while a variety of feelings engulfed her. To travel; see a little of the world, even if it was only a few hundred miles across the North Sea, meet people—she would need new clothes. She said in a bemused voice, 'Aren't you coming back here?'

'Of course. Most of my work is here.'

'Surely you can't write a book and operate and lecture, not all at once?'

'Yes, I can, and I shall expect you to type notes, letters and whatever, answer the phone, check my appointments and type my book. Miss Payne could and did; I see no reason why you shouldn't do it too— you're a good deal younger, for a start.'

Serena frowned. Miss Payne was obviously nearing retirement age, so to be told that she was a good deal younger wasn't much of a compliment. Dr ter Faulen read the frown unerringly. 'You are twenty-five, half a lifetime younger than Muriel...'

'Muriel? Oh, Miss Payne. Well, may I think about it? I mean, I'd have to...' She stopped suddenly and a look of dismay on her face caused him to go back to his chair and sit down again. His 'Well?' was uttered with just the right amount of interest and sympathy.

'I can't. Truly, I can't. You see, there's Mother...'

'Widowed?' and when she nodded, 'She is ill?'

'No, just—well, just—delicate.'

'Why is that? She has a heart condition? A chest condition? Diabetes? Arthritis?' He fired the words at her and she blinked.

'No, no, nothing like that. She suffers from nerves, she finds it difficult to do things...'

'Housework, shopping and so forth?'

'Yes.'

He sighed gently. Selfish widows with loving daughters were still only too common, and this small, neat girl with the beautiful eyes deserved something more in life. He said slowly, 'In that case we might kill two birds with one stone. Miss Payne, when she accompanied me, had lodgings close to the hospital and came to work just as she did here. There is no reason why your mother should not accompany you and stay at these same lodgings. I shall be in Amsterdam for most of the time, and there is plenty to see and do there.'

'She doesn't understand Dutch—nor do I.'

'My dear girl, almost everyone in Holland speaks English.'

He watched excited hope chase away the dismay. 'Oh, do you really mean that?'

'I always say what I mean. Go home and talk it over with your mother and let me know tomorrow morning.'

He got up for a second time and this time, with a nod and a casual goodnight, went away.

She finished her work, tidied her desk and wondered what she should do with the sheaf of letters waiting to be signed. She was hesitating whether to phone the consultants' room when the head porter rang up. She was to leave everything with him and Dr ter Feulen would collect his letters later.

She handed in her work and hurried to catch her bus, rehearsing what she would say to her mother. Her spirits sank as she neared home—her mother would never consent to the upheaval in her well-ordered life. She let herself into her home, resigned to disappointment but all the same determined to do her best to persuade her parent that a change of scene would do her a great deal of good.

She cast off her outdoor things in the hall and went into the sitting-room.

Her mother was sitting at her writing desk, pen poised. 'There you are, darling. What splendid news— I've had such a long chat on the telephone with Dr ter Feulen. He sounds a delightful man—apologised for keeping you so late and told me how much he depends upon your assistance. And this marvellous job you're to take over, and going to Holland too! I can hardly wait. He is of the opinion that a change of scene is just what is needed for someone as delicate as I am.'

Her mother paused for breath and Serena said in a voice she strove to keep calm, 'He rang up? So you know all about it? And you'd like to go? It won't be too much for you, Mother?'

'Certainly not! It will probably take a few days for me to get over the journey, but I will willingly tire myself out for you, darling. I'm making a list of the clothes I shall need... Have you had supper? I've been so busy... Could you get us something now? I must keep up what strength I have.' She looked at Serena. 'You look a bit white, dear. You need a meal too, I dare say.'

'Mother, I haven't said I'd take the job yet.'

Her mother gave her an outraged look. 'Darling, why ever not? What a funny little thing you are! Why ever not?'

'I wasn't sure if you would like the idea.'

Her mother laughed. 'Darling, I love the idea! Tell me, how old is this Dr ter Feulen?'

'I don't know—about thirty-five or -six, I should think.'

'Married?'

'I've no idea.' A fib, and she wasn't sure why she had said it.

'Well, we're bound to get to know a lot of people in Amsterdam. Pour me a glass of sherry, will you, Serena? I need the stimulant.'

There was little opportunity to think her own thoughts that evening. Mrs Proudfoot made plans, discussed clothes and speculated as to the pleasures in store.

'Mother, it won't be quite like a holiday,' Serena warned carefully. 'I shall be working very hard every day, so you'll be on your own for a great deal of the time.'

'I'm on my own every day now, darling, and deadly boring it is too. If only I had your health and strength.'

They got to bed at last, and Serena lay awake for a long time wondering if she had done the right thing, or rather if the right thing had been done for her, for she had had little say in the matter.

She wasn't sure if she was pleased at the doctor's intervention either. He had forced her hand and there was no going back now, for her mother was determined to go. All the same, when she saw him in the morning she would tell him that he had no right to interfere. On this firm resolution she at last slept.

CHAPTER TWO

SERENA was still firmly resolved to speak her mind to the doctor when she went to work in the morning. It was unfortunate that it wasn't until the end of the day that she had the opportunity to do so.

She was on the way to the side entrance she normally used when she came face to face with him. She slid to a halt and said briskly, 'Oh, good, I wanted to see you, Dr ter Feulen.'

He stood in front of her, blocking the way. 'Ah, Miss Proudfoot, should I be greatly flattered at your eagerness to see me again?' He paused and looked at her earnest, rather cross face. 'No, that is too much to expect. I have annoyed you?'

She suspected that he was laughing at her. 'I think it was most—most unfair of you to telephone my mother before I'd had a chance to talk to her. I haven't said I'll take the job, have I? So what right have you to—to—to...!'

'Interfere?' he suggested helpfully. 'Meddle in your affairs? No right at all. My intentions were purely selfish. After some years of Muriel's calm acceptance of my ill humour, impatience and bad handwriting, I have been terrified of engaging her successor. Who knows what foibles she might have? A desire to finish her work at the correct time, an inability to ignore my bad temper, a desire to answer back pertly as well as a failure to spell correctly.' He smiled at her and she found herself smiling back. 'You are the nearest thing to Miss Payne that I have met.'

A kind of compliment, Serena decided, and warmed just a little towards him. But only for a moment. 'You are unobtrusive,' he went on. 'There is nothing about you to distract my attention from my work——'

'Just like Miss Payne,' said Serena through her teeth.

'Exactly so, and I must remind you that a change of scene may be a help to your mother and aid her to overcome her ill health. She seemed delighted at the idea.'

Serena, hanging on to politeness by the skin of her teeth, agreed that that was so.

He smiled again, looking faintly smug, and she longed to refuse the job out of hand, but the thought of her mother stopped her. She said reluctantly, 'Very well, I'll work for you, Dr ter Feulen.'

'Splendid.' He glanced at his watch. 'And since I have kept you talking I will drive you home and make the acquaintance of your mother.'

She opened her mouth to protest, and closed it again. Getting the better of him was like getting the better of a feather mattress with a solid core of steel.

Her annoyance was very slightly mitigated by the pleasure of riding in a Bentley, but not sufficient for her to do more than answer his casual talk with monosyllables. She opened her front door and said with false politeness, 'Do come in, Dr ter Feulen,' and flattened herself against the wall to allow his considerable bulk to get past her.

Her mother's voice sounded thinly from the sitting-room. 'Serena? You're late again, darling—I hope you've thought of something nice for my supper, I'm far too exhausted to do anything about it. Perhaps a glass of sherry...?'

The doctor glanced at Serena's face, which was a little pale and weary after a day's work. He had been right in his surmise about her mother; a selfish woman, not unkind but quite uncaring of anyone but herself. He put a large hand on her shoulder and smiled a little, and she stifled an urge to fling herself on to his big chest and have a good cry.

'Come and meet Mother,' she invited in a small controlled voice.

The doctor had charm. He also had guile and the self-assurance to deal with difficult situations without anyone else realising the fact. Within half an hour, over a glass of sherry, he had arranged matters exactly to his liking, with Mrs Proudfoot agreeing to every word, and although he had included Serena in the conversation she was bound to admit later that she had been given no opportunity to say anything much. The whole matter had been settled by the time he took his leave.

The moment he had gone Mrs Proudfoot went back to her desk. 'My dear,' she exclaimed excitedly, 'this is all so thrilling—and so little time! I shall need several more dresses. Be a darling and start the supper while I go over my list.'

Over supper Mrs Proudfoot discussed the trip. She had for the moment overlooked the fact that it was to be no social round. She was envisaging days packed with outings, theatres and little dinners. In none of these plans did Serena figure.

'Mother,' said Serena, matter-of-factly, 'I don't suppose it will be quite as exciting as you suppose. We don't know a soul in Holland——' she ignored her mother's quick 'Dr ter Feulen,' '—I shall be away all day, and I imagine that the lodgings the doctor has in mind will be fairly quiet.'

Her mother made a pouting face. 'Darling, you are so prosaic! It's the chance of a lifetime, and you might at least be pleased about it and not spoil my pleasure by boring on about your work.' She patted Serena's arm and smiled beguilingly. 'Serena, don't mind me saying this, but I am your mother and I want the best for you. Take care you don't become a prig— sometimes you're too good to be true.'

She gave a tinkling laugh. 'There, don't I sound horrid? But I say it for your own good. You don't want to spend all your life in a dull office, do you?' She patted her carefully arranged curls. 'Besides, I might marry again.'

Serena, the memory of whose father was still a well-hidden sorrow, poured coffee and handed her mother a cup. 'Anyone I know?' she asked.

'Well, no, dear, but I flatter myself that I'm still fairly youthful as well as being good company, and who knows, I might meet someone I like in Holland.'

Perhaps she had done the wrong thing in agreeing to take on the new job, thought Serena worriedly, and when, some days later, she met Dr ter Feulen at the hospital, she begged a moment of his time, and when he paused impatiently with a politely curt, 'Well, what can I do for you?' she wasted no time in coming to the point.

'I don't think it will help Mother at all to go to Holland,' she said, not mincing matters. 'She leads such a quiet life, and she's delicate . . .'

'Since you were worried about your mother's health, Miss Proudfoot, I made a point of visiting her. And as we are speaking plainly, I must tell you that I formed the opinion that there is nothing the matter with your mother. Her health would improve immediately if she were to take up some occupation—housework, cooking, voluntary work of some kind. If that sounds to you harsh I do not mean it to be so. I have no doubt that during the weeks she will be in Amsterdam she will find friends and perhaps involve herself in some activity or other.' He glanced at his watch. 'Forgive me, I'm due in theatre.'

Not a very satisfactory conversation, reflected Serena.

She was kept busy at home as well as at work. She had been unable to discover for how long they would be away, but all the same all the particulars appertaining to the closing of the house had to be attended to, arrangements had to be made at the bank so that her mother's pension could be transferred and passports renewed, which didn't leave much time over for her own shopping.

It was October now and, although the pleasant autumn weather still held, there was a nip in the air and yet it might not be cold enough for a winter coat. She dug into her savings and got herself a short wool coat in a pleasing shade of aubergine and found a pleated skirt in a matching check. An outsize cream sweater and a couple of blouses completed the outfit and would, she considered, stand her in good stead for the duration of her stay in Holland. A dark green jersey dress, by no means new but a useful addition to her wardrobe, and a brown velveteen dress, very plain but nicely cut, a raincoat, a pair of court shoes and a sensible pair of walking shoes would, she considered, be sufficient for her needs, although at the last minute she added a thick tweed skirt and a rather elderly anorak as well as woolly gloves and a woolly cap. Mrs Dunn had told her that Miss Payne, on a previous visit to Holland, had suffered badly from nipped fingers and cold ears.

Her mother's wardrobe was much more varied and very large and certainly there was enough to cover the entire winter, but Serena forbore from remarking on this after a first attempt which had ended in her mother saying pettishly that it was obvious that she wasn't wanted and she might as well stay at home alone as she always was. 'After all I've done for you,' she ended, and Serena, soothing her back to a good humour, sighed to herself. A good and loving daughter, nevertheless sometimes she longed to have her freedom; to lead her own life and make friends of her own age. She had friends, of course, but nowadays they were either married and living miles away or living on their own with splendid jobs entailing a good deal of travelling and meeting important people. From time to time they had suggested to her that she might share a flat and find a job, but her mother had made that impossible; not by standing in her way but by becoming pale and silent and pathetically cheerful about the future. She would, of course, manage, she told Serena. She would sell their home, of course, for she could never manage to run it alone, and she would find one of those flats where there was a warden to look after one if one became ill and didn't wish to worry one's family. There wouldn't be much money, of course, without Serena's contribution, but she had no doubt that she would contrive. And all this said with a brave smile and a wistful droop that wrung Serena's heart and squashed any hopes of a life of her own.

It was several days after her conversation with Dr ter Feulen that she found a letter on her desk when she arrived at work—a typed letter setting out the day on which she and her mother were to travel and from where. They were to fly, and she would receive their tickets in due course. They would be met at Schiphol airport and taken to the boarding-house where rooms had been reserved for them. She was to report for work on the following morning at eight o'clock. Her timetable would be at the boarding-house. He had signed it M. Dijkstra ter Feulen.

When Serena got home she showed her mother the letter. Mrs Proudfoot was put out. 'I can't see why we couldn't go over to Holland in his car! He must be going at about the same time. With my poor health all this business of getting to Heathrow and flying to Amsterdam is bound to upset my nerves.'

Serena held her tongue. The doctor had made it plain that he considered that her mother was as fit as the next woman, but he had spoken in confidence. Perhaps when the time was right, he would suggest that she should change her lifestyle. 'Possibly he'll travel at an awkward time,' she suggested tactfully.

It was two days before they were due to leave that she heard quite by accident that he had already left the hospital. 'Left late last night,' Mrs Dunn told her, 'and he's not expected back for several weeks, so Theatre Sister tells me, although there are several cases lined up for him before Christmas.' She eyed Serena curiously. 'Don't you know how long you'll be gone?'

'Not exactly. It depends on his work in Holland.'

'Oh, well, you're a lucky girl, stepping into Miss Payne's shoes and getting a chance to travel a bit. Mind you, he expects a lot from his secretary. Miss Payne was with him for quite a time, it'll be hard to live up to her standards...'

Not a very cheering prospect, but one Serena was prepared to ignore. However hard she would have to work she would be in a foreign country and she intended to make the most of it. Moreover, from the moment she stepped on to Dutch soil, she would be earning considerably more money. If they were back home for Christmas, and she was sure that they would be, they would be able to go to a theatre or two, and buy all the extras which made all the difference at the festive season, perhaps have a day shopping at her mother's favourite stores... 'I'll do my best,' she assured Mrs Dunn cheerfully.

Mrs Proudfoot had insisted on a taxi to Heathrow, an expense which Serena could well have done without, and, once there, her mother complained about having time to wait for their flight, the coffee, the lack of comfortable seats and how exhausted she was. Serena, occupied with luggage, tickets and passports, bit back impatient words, assured her mother that once they were on the plane everything would be fine, and so it was. The flight was brief, the coffee and biscuits they were offered passed the time very nicely and in no time at all they were at Schiphol.

There was a tricky delay while Serena fetched their bags from the carousel and a few anxious moments wondering if they would be met, quickly forgotten when an elderly man approached them. 'Mrs Proudfoot and Miss Proudfoot? Dr Dijkstra ter

Feulen wished me to meet you. My name is Cor, if you will please follow me.'

He was a sturdily built man and made light of their suitcases, walking ahead of them out of the airport entrance and leading them to a dark blue Jaguar. He opened the car door and ushered them in, put their bags in the boot and got into the driver's seat.

'A drive of half an hour,' he told them, and started the car.

Mrs Proudfoot had stopped complaining, for there was nothing to complain about—indeed, she became quite animated as they neared Amsterdam, exclaiming over the churches, old houses and canals once they had gone through the modern encircling suburbs. Cor stopped finally in a narrow street with blocks of flats interspersed with solid houses, built of red brick round the turn of the century. It was to one of these that he led them, rang the bell and waited with them until the door opened. The woman who answered it was middle-aged and stout, with a pleasant face and small beady eyes.

'The English ladies,' she greeted them. 'Welcome. Come in, please.'

Her English was as good as Cor's but heavily accented. She spoke to him in their own tongue and he went to the car and fetched the luggage and put it in the hall. 'I wish you a pleasant stay,' he told them, and Mrs Proudfoot smiled graciously.

Serena shook his hand and thanked him. 'It was so nice to be met by someone who speaks English; it all seems a bit strange, and we are most grateful.' She started to open her purse, but he laid a large beefy hand on hers.

'No, no, miss. That is not necessary—the doctor has arranged all...'

He gave her a beaming smile, said something to their landlady and went away.

'So, now we will go to your rooms. My name is Mevrouw Blom and I am glad to know you. Come...'

Serena picked up one of their cases and Mevrouw Blom took the other two, while Mrs Proudfoot carried her umbrella. The stairs leading from the narrow hall were steep, covered in serviceable carpeting and led to a narrow landing. Mevrouw Blom opened two of the three doors and waved Serena and her mother into the rooms. They were identical as to furniture: a bed, a table under the narrow window with a small mirror, a small easy chair, a small table by the bed and a large, old-fashioned wardrobe. The floors were wooden, with rugs by the beds and under the windows. There were overhead lights as well as bedside lamps and a radiator against one wall in each room. 'You will tidy yourselves,' said Mevrouw Blom cheerfully, 'and then return to the room below and take coffee.'

'The bathroom?' asked Serena.

'Ah, yes—there is a shower-room.' The third door was opened to show a tiled shower-room with a washbasin.

Mevrouw Blom went back downstairs and Mrs Proudfoot turned to Serena. 'I thought it would have been a hotel,' she complained peevishly. 'It's nothing but a cheap boarding-house!'

'Mother, it's clean and warm and quite nicely furnished, and you mustn't forget that the doctor is paying for both of us; he had to pay for me, I know, but he needn't have done so for you.' She kissed her mother. 'Let's tidy ourselves and go downstairs.'

Mevrouw Blom was waiting for them and ushered them into a large room which opened into a second smaller room at the back of the house. Both rooms were well furnished with comfortable chairs, small tables, and, in the smaller of the rooms, several tables were laid for a meal. Mrs Proudfoot brightened at the sight of the TV in one corner and the closed stove in the larger of the rooms. She sat down in a chair close to it while Mrs Blom poured coffee and handed cups with small sugary biscuits. The coffee was delicious and she sipped it. Perhaps it wasn't too bad...

'I have a letter for you, miss,' said Mevrouw Blom, 'from Dr Dijkstra ter Feulen. He tells me you go to work at eight o'clock, therefore there is breakfast for you at half-past seven. The hospital is five minutes' walking—I will show you. You eat your supper here each evening and if you are late that is OK.' She chuckled. 'Miss Payne, when she was here, was sometimes late, but that is not important.'

She poured more coffee and Serena, with a murmured excuse, sat down near the window to read her letter.

It was a cold businesslike missive, but she hadn't expected anything else. She was to present herself at the porter's lodge at eight o'clock, where she would be taken to the room where she was to work. She was to be prepared to go to the wards, outpatients' clinic or the theatre block, and she should familiarise herself with the hospital at the earliest opportunity. Here her normal working day would end at five o'clock with an hour for lunch, but these hours might be varied. As hers, M. Dijkstra ter Feulen. At least she d the unreadable scrawl was his.

She folded the letter and put it back in its envelope. He might have expressed the hope that she would like her work, or something equally civil. He was not a man to waste words on polite nothings, however. To her mother's enquiry as to the contents of the envelope, she replied in her calm way that it only contained instructions as to her work. 'I shall be away all day, Mother, so for the time being don't plan anything for the evenings, as Dr ter Feulen mentions that I may need to work late. I shall know more when I've been there for a day or two.'

Her mother was prepared to argue, but at that moment several people came into the room and Mevrouw Blom with them.

'These ladies and gentlemen are also staying here,' she explained. 'I make them known to you now.'

There were two middle-aged ladies, stout and well dressed, who smiled broadly, shook hands and murmured.

'They tell their names,' said Mevrouw Blom. 'Mevrouw Lagerveld and Mevrouw van Til, and the gentlemen...'

Mijnheer van Til shook hands and spoke, to Serena's relief, in English. 'I am charmed, now I may exercise my English?' and Mijnheer Lagerveld, shaking hands in his turn, essayed a few words with the excuse that his English was poor.

'Here we have a surprise,' chimed in Mevrouw Blom, looking pleased with herself. 'This is Mr Harding, from England, who stays with me while he studies the old houses of Amsterdam.'

He was a thin man of middle height, nice-looking with grey hair and mild blue eyes. Serena guessed him to be in his early sixties.

'This is a most pleasant surprise,' he observed as he shook hands. 'I hope you'll be staying for some time.'

Mrs Proudfoot smiled charmingly. 'Oh, I think so. My daughter is to work at the hospital for some weeks and I've come with her—my doctor considered a change of scene might improve my health.'

She looked round her and sighed with pleasure. Perhaps it wasn't such a cheap boarding-house after all. Here was company, people she could talk to, and Mr Harding looked quite promising...

Serena left them presently and went upstairs to unpack her things, and then, since her mother had done nothing about her own luggage, unpacked for her, too, hung everything tidily away in the wardrobe and went back to her room to read the doctor's letter again. If she had hoped to read a little warmth into it she failed.

The evening meal was at six o'clock—a substantial one of soup, meatballs, vegetables and potatoes, followed by blancmange. Mrs Proudfoot, who normally pecked at the kind of invalid diet she had devised for herself, ate everything, explaining to Mr Harding that after their tiring journey she needed to keep up her strength. It surprised and pleased Serena to see her mother so animated, and indeed, when she suggested that she must be tired and an early night might be advisable, Mrs Proudfoot said prettily that she was enjoying the company far too much to leave it so early and advised Serena to go to bed herself. 'For I dare say you'll have a busy day, darling.' She put up her cheek for Serena to kiss. 'I'll see you to-morrow evening, you leave far too early in the morning.' She smiled around the room. 'I sleep badly and usually doze off just as everyone else is getting up!'

Serena wished everyone goodnight and climbed the steep stairs once more, had a shower, set her alarm clock, and then climbed into bed. It was altogether a relief that her mother seemed happy, and it was providential that there was the English Mr Harding for her to talk to. He would probably have the leisure to spend some time with her; at least he would be there to talk to her at meals. Serena burrowed her mousy head into the large square pillow and went to sleep.

When she went downstairs soon after seven o'clock the next morning she found Mevrouw Blom waiting for her. The rooms were spotless, the tables laid for breakfast, the stove already lighted.

'You sleep well?' asked Mevrouw Blom. 'I bring coffee and rolls if you will sit.'

Serena wasn't very hungry, she was too excited for that, but she managed to eat the boiled egg and a roll and cheese and drink the contents of the coffee-pot. No one had mentioned arrangements for her midday meal. Perhaps she was expected to go into the town for it, or return to Mevrouw Blom, but at the moment her lunch was the least important of her thoughts; she was more concerned in getting to the hospital and being where Dr ter Feulen expected her to be by eight o'clock.

The hospital was very close by, indeed she could see it looming over the housetops as she went out of the front door, and once there, with ten minutes to spare, she went to the porter's lodge and gave her name.

The porter was elderly with a craggy face and a neat fringe of hair around his bald head. He answered her good morning with a remark in his own tongue and picked up the telephone. Since the conversation meant nothing to her, Serena took a look around her. The hospital entrance was imposing, with a paved floor and a wide sweeping staircase opposite the doors. They led to a landing lined with lifts as far as she could see, and then branched on either side to the floor above.

'Wait, if you please,' said the porter in very bad English, and turned back to sorting the letters.

So she waited, one eye on the enormous clock above the stairs; it was five minutes to eight and she didn't care to arrive late on her first morning. The minute hand had moved to four minutes before a stout woman with iron-grey hair and a severe expression came from somewhere at the back of the hall.

'Miss Proudfoot—good morning. You are to come with me.' She looked Serena over. 'You are a good deal younger than Miss Payne...' She held out a hand. 'Juffrouw Staal.'

'Serena Proudfoot,' said Serena, and smiled hopefully. But all Juffrouw Staal did was to nod her head briskly and lead the way to the back of the hall and through a door. There was a stone staircase beyond it and she started up it, saying over her shoulder,

'You will come this way each day, you will not need to speak to the porter.'

They climbed to the third floor and went through a swing-door into a wide passage with rooms opening from it on either side. Almost at the end of it Juffrouw Staal stopped. 'Dr ter Feulen comes to this room to dictate his letters and give you his instructions. You will also be required to go to the wards and clinics if he wishes to record some of his cases.'

She indicated the desk and chair set under the window. 'You will go for your coffee at ten o'clock. The canteen is on the ground floor—someone will show you. You will also lunch there at fifteen minutes past twelve. You may have ten minutes for tea, and that is at half-past three. The cloakrooms are at the end of this corridor.'

Serena thanked her. 'You speak English awfully well,' she said.

Miss Staal unbent very slightly. 'I have lived in your country for a year or so. You will be here only a short time, but I advise you to learn a few basic phrases as soon as possible.'

She nodded and went away, leaving Serena to take the cover off her typewriter, look into the drawers and cupboards and make sure that her pencils were sharpened, and, that done, she went to the window to look out over the neighbouring streets. It was a grey morning and there was a mean wind, but the city looked interesting from where she stood, looking down on to its roofs.

'I suppose I stay here until someone comes, and let's hope that's soon—he might turn nasty if I'm late.' She had spoken out loud, as she so often did when she was alone, and a slight sound made her turn round in a hurry.

Dr ter Feulen had come into the room. He gave her an unsmiling good morning and added, 'Since you're not late I can see no reason to turn nasty. You have a poor opinion of me, Miss Proudfoot.'

She had gone pink, but she didn't avoid his eye. 'No, not really, it's just that I'm a bit nervous of doing the wrong thing, and to be late would be such a very bad start.'

He nodded carelessly. 'You are comfortable at Mevrouw Blom's house?'

'Oh, very, thank you, and Mother is so pleased. There are other people there who speak English and an English gentleman . . .' She stopped because he was looking impatient. She asked quickly, 'What do you wish me to do first, sir?'

He stood looking at her and she wondered if there was something wrong with her. She had left the house as neat as a new pin, but the hurried climb up the stairs might have loosened her tidy head of hair, or was her blouse rumpled? She surveyed her person with an anxious eye, relieved at last to hear him say, 'No, there's nothing wrong, Miss Proudfoot. And must I call you that? You won't object to being called Serena?'

'Not in the least, sir.'

'Then let us make a tour of the hospital so that when you are sent for you don't take all day to get there.'

She said crossly, quite forgetting to whom she was speaking, 'You do have a most unfortunate way of making me feel inadequate! I'm sure I'm quite capable of finding my way around without anyone's help.'

'Oh, undoubtedly. But all the same, perhaps you will be good enough to come with me now.'

She went out of the room with something of a flounce, not seeing his smile, and after ten minutes of traipsing up and down stairs and along corridors which all looked alike, she was forced to admit that without him she would have been hopelessly lost. She took care to look where she went; the theatre block was on the top floor and Outpatients was on the ground floor at the back of the hospital. She was introduced to the ward sisters, and it wasn't until they were back in the office where she was to work that she realised how difficult it would have been to find her way around the vast place without a guide. She said apologetically, 'I'm sorry I was so rude. It was kind of you to show me round—I would have got hopelessly lost.'

The doctor nodded, unsmiling. 'Indeed you would, and I might have turned nasty!' He saw the look on her face and said hastily, 'No—it is I who am sorry. I had no reason to say that. I think we shall get on very well together. Let us begin as we mean to go on. I have a clinic in ten minutes' time. Bring your notebook and pencil—there's a long morning's work ahead of us.' He nodded again, but this time he smiled.

He was really rather nice, she decided, watching his broad back disappear along the corridor.

That evening, reviewing her day, Serena decided that she hadn't done so badly. It had been very like working at the Royal, and although the doctor had spoken Dutch to his patients he had detailed his notes in English, and he and his registrar had spoken together in that language with as much ease as if they were speaking their own tongue. Serena had been nervous at first, but by the end of the morning she had found her feet and had gone down to the canteen for her lunch with two of the other hospital clerks and had quite enjoyed herself. She had spent the afternoon typing up the notes, typed up the details of an operation the doctor had performed that afternoon, this time from a tape recorder, and handed the whole lot

to him when he came to the office just after half-past
five. She had asked him if he wanted her for anything
else and he had replied that no, he thought not, she
had done sufficient for her first day.

'I shall be operating in the morning,' he told her,
'but I'll send someone up with my letters and a couple
of tapes. Have them ready by two o'clock, will you?'

They had wished each other goodnight and she had
gone back to Mevrouw Blom's house to find the
evening meal already eaten, although she was given
soup, pork chops, *zuurkool* and delicious floury
potatoes by an attentive Mevrouw Blom, followed by
ice-cream and coffee, while everyone else sat in the
sitting-room. Her mother had been remarkably
cheerful, full of her day, and beyond a perfunctory
question or two as to what Serena had done, she had
little interest in it. But Serena hadn't minded, it was
a relief to find that her mother was actually enjoying
herself. There was no trace of boredom and no com-
plaints of headaches or tiredness—indeed, she was the
life and soul of everyone there, and barely noticed
when Serena after an hour or so slipped away to her
bed. It was nice to see her mother so happy, she
thought sleepily, and that nice Mr Harding had been
very kind, taking her mother into the heart of the city
and showing her where all the best shops were. Serena,
curled up in her comfortable bed, went to sleep.

By the end of the week she had to admit that she was
enjoying herself. It was all work, but interesting, and
she hardly noticed that she had very little leisure. Dr
ter Feulen was a glutton for work; when he wasn't
operating he was dictating letters, giving lectures or
examining students. Serena made copious notes, typed

them neatly and left them each evening with Juffrouw Staal. She saw the doctor each day, but beyond wanting to know in a rather impatient manner if she was all right, he had nothing of a personal nature to say to her. She returned to the cheerful haven of Mevrouw Blom's house each evening, tired and hungry but satisfied that she had done a good day's work and delighted to find that her mother was enjoying herself. Mr Harding had taken her under his elderly wing and each evening she recounted to Serena the various pleasures of her day. She didn't want to know about Serena's; she dismissed it as boring, and beyond a fleeting concern that Serena didn't seem to have much time to herself, she had no comment to make.

'Well, I'll be free on Saturday,' said Serena.

'Oh, will you, darling? You'll love to potter round the shops. Mr Harding is taking me to Utrecht—there are some patrician houses there he wants to see. He says I have a great eye for architecture...'

Serena swallowed disappointment. She had been looking forward to a day sightseeing with her mother, but all she said in her sensible way was, 'That sounds fun. I'm so glad you're enjoying yourself, Mother, and you look years younger.'

Mrs Proudfoot peered into the small looking-glass. 'Yes, I do, don't I?' she agreed complacently, and added without much interest, 'You're not working too hard, are you, darling?'

Serena assured her that she wasn't.

She was asked that question again on the following morning, but by the doctor. She assured him that she had never felt better, and he gave her a quizzical look.

'You are free tomorrow and Sunday, so you and your mother will be able to explore.'

'Well, actually, she's going out with Mr Harding who's at Mevrouw Blom's—they're going to Utrecht to look at old houses.'

'And you?'

'Me? Oh, I'll look at the shops and wander about.' She had spoken in a cheerful and matter-of-fact voice, but something in her face made him give her a thoughtful look.

He said, 'There is quite a lot to see in Amsterdam,' and Serena said too quickly,

'Oh, yes, I know, I'm looking forward to it.'

He went away and she started her day's work, resolutely determined not to feel sorry for herself.

She found herself unwillingly tidying her desk that evening, knowing that she wouldn't be at it for two days. She felt secure while she was working, and she was beginning to make the acquaintance of other girls who worked along the corridor; they were friendly and kind and they all spoke English of sorts. Serena was last, as usual. She turned off the lights as she went, ran down the stairs and out of the side door and into the street, then hurried along the pavement to Mevrouw Blom's house, watched by the doctor, sitting in his car, waiting for a gap in the traffic.

CHAPTER THREE

SERENA got up early the next morning, had her breakfast with Mevrouw Blom, tidied her room and went to say good morning to her mother.

'Darling, why so early?' asked Mrs Proudfoot. 'Are you going somewhere nice?'

'I'm going to explore. Mr Harding is having his breakfast—what time are you going?'

Mrs Proudfoot took a close look at her face and gave a satisfied nod. 'I must go down now, we're leaving by half-past nine. Come down with me and pour my coffee, darling.'

So Serena in her new jacket and skirt, silk blouse and sensible low-heeled shoes, since she intended to walk a great deal, went back to the dining-room and poured her mother's coffee, then made small talk with Mr Harding and the Lagervelds and the van Tils. She had got to her feet with a cheerful remark about going on her way when Mevrouw Blom opened the door.

'Serena—here you have a visitor.' She beamed around the room and stood aside as Dr ter Feulen walked past her.

The size of him made the room all at once smaller. Serena, who had never seen him in anything but exquisitely tailored dark grey suits and long white hospital coats, thought the tweeds he was wearing made him look younger, but this reflection was swallowed up in the supposition that he wanted her to go back to the hospital and do some work.

His greeting to everyone in the room was polite and genial, and Mrs Proudfoot exclaimed, 'Dr ter Feulen, how delightful——'

He cut her short with practised ease. 'I'm glad to see you looking so well.' He rested his cool look on Serena. 'I intend to show you something of Amsterdam, Serena.' He paused and added, 'Unless you had any other plans?' His deep voice held a note of disbelief that she might have any ideas of her own, and she opened her mouth to refuse while at the same time a small voice inside her head reminded her that here was a chance to go sightseeing without any effort on her part, and, what was even nicer, she wouldn't be on her own. The loneliness she had been feeling ever since her mother had told her that she would be spending the day with Mr Harding melted away under his look.

She heard herself say with just the right tone of pleasure, 'No, I didn't make any special plans, and I should enjoy seeing something of Amsterdam.'

He nodded. 'Good. Let us go, if you are ready.'

'There's something I need from my room...' She raced upstairs to repowder her nose and deplore its beakiness, and tidy the already tidy head of mousy hair. There was a bottle of Femme somewhere... She found it and sprayed her person, then raced down again.

They bade everyone goodbye, Serena in a quiet composed voice masking excitement, the doctor gravely, very appreciative of the faint aura of Femme around Serena.

Outside on the pavement she paused. 'I thought you'd come to ask me to do some work... Do you really want to take me sightseeing?'

He assured her gravely that it would give him pleasure to show her something of the city. 'We have both been working very hard,' he pointed out. 'Besides, it will make further sightseeing trips for you somewhat easier.' He stowed her into the Bentley. 'Although,' he went on smoothly, 'Mr Harding may invite you as well as your mother?'

Serena turned to look at him as he got in beside her. 'Oh, I shouldn't think so. Two's company, three's none, you know. He and Mother get on so well together, she really is having a lovely time.'

'Then we must see if we can also have a lovely time.' He drove off, and Serena sat back against the comforting leather seat. She was still very surprised at the doctor's appearance, but she intended to enjoy every minute of her unexpected treat. He must have a reason, she reflected, and thought she had discovered it when she heard him say abruptly, 'I shall be going to den Haag on Monday. I shall be there for several days, operating and in consultation. You will accompany me, of course. You will be given a room in the hospital where I shall be working. Your work will be the same as it is here.'

She said in her quiet way, 'Very well, Doctor. Mother will stay here?'

'Why not? She seems happy. She sees very little of you?'

'Well, yes. What I mean is, no, she doesn't see a great deal of me.'

'In that case it would be kinder to leave her at Mevrouw Blom's, would it not? You will probably be back by the weekend.' He sounded uninterested.

'Why did you ask me out?' Serena asked abruptly.

'Muriel and I invariably had a few hours of sight-seeing when we came here,' he told her blandly. Which was the kind of answer she might have expected from him. Only it wasn't an answer really.

He had driven into the heart of the city, and Serena, her head swivelling from side to side in order not to miss anything, asked, 'Is that the Munttoren?'

'Yes. You shall see it presently. We will park the car first and have some coffee.'

He turned into Nieuwe Doelenstraat and stopped before the Hotel de l'Europe.

'Here?' asked Serena.

'Here.' He unfastened her safety-belt, got out and opened her door, then marched her to the hotel entrance, stopping to say something to the doorman.

'Your car?' queried Serena, shocked at the way he had left it there without so much as locking its doors.

'That's taken care of,' said the doctor, ushering her into an extremely comfortable foyer with a large lounge beyond. 'They'll keep it here for me until I want it.'

He sat her down at a small table by the window with a view of the river and beckoned a waiter, ordered coffee and took off his car coat.

'We shall return to Amsterdam at the start of next week,' he announced. 'I shall be at the hospital here for two or three days and then I have to go to appointments in Leeuwarden. These will keep me there for a weekend or more. You will accompany me, of course.'

Serena poured the coffee and handed him a cup. 'What about Mother?' she asked urgently. 'I can't leave her.'

He sat back comfortably. 'But you leave her every day, do you not? And it seems that she is perfectly happy without your company.'

'What a very nasty thing to say,' said Serena. 'You know as well as I do——'

'Probably better,' he said suavely, ignoring her cross look. 'You don't wish to believe me, but your mother is as fit as you or I. I suspect that she has been bored and with nothing to do has invented ill health. And don't look at me like that; your mother is a charming woman and still pretty. She should marry again.'

Serena drew an indignant breath. 'Well, of all the things to say, I never——'

He handed his cup for more coffee. 'You strike me as being an honest girl, Serena, so give me an honest answer.' He smiled at her eyes widened by his charm and warmth. 'Your mother is happy in this Mr Harding's company, is she not? And were you asked to go with them today?'

'Yes,' said Serena slowly, 'and no, I wasn't.'

'Good. Now, having cleared up that small problem, let us enjoy ourselves.'

He plunged her into the Muntplein, pausing to point out its history, and then swept her on into the Kalverstraat, a narrow, long street lined with shops and bustling with people. Serena's little beaky nose twitched with pleasure at the sight of the small elegant shops and the doctor, waiting patiently, let her peer into their windows until she glanced at his impassive face. 'Oh, sorry, I dare say shops bore you—only I haven't seen any. . .'

He took her arm. 'There are some splendid shops in den Haag. We're going in here.' He pointed to the street sign. 'Begijnsteeg—it leads to some almshouses, the oldest are fourteenth century, and there's a church which we gave to your country in the seventeenth century.'

The Begijnhof was beautiful and serene under the autumn sky, its small houses crowded together in a circle round the church. Serena stood very still, feeling its peace. 'Who lives here now?' she asked softly.

'Respectable widows and old maiden ladies. You like it?'

He was watching her face alight with pleasure. 'It makes you feel contented,' she said.

'At last we are able to agree upon something.' He led her back into the Kalverstraat. 'Now we will visit the Rembrandthuis. It is in the Jewish quarter, and there are other interesting buildings there.'

The museum appeared closed when they arrived at it, but the doctor beat a tattoo on its door and it was opened immediately. He urged Serena inside. 'This is Mijnheer de Vries, the caretaker. The museum is closed, but he has kindly allowed us to look round for half an hour.'

Mijnheer de Vries shook hands, had a short talk about nothing in particular and took himself off.

'Is he a friend of yours?' asked Serena.

'Yes. Now come and look at these etchings...'

Half an hour later Mijnheer de Vries joined them. 'You need a day, two days,' he said regretfully.

'But half an hour is better than nothing at all,' said the doctor. 'I'm grateful...'

Mijnheer de Vries broke into English. 'Grateful? It is I who am grateful—you saved my wife's life...'

'She is well?'

'Almost her old self, thanks to you, Doctor.'

'That is good news. Now we must go. We're cramming several days' sightseeing into a few hours.'

They all shook hands again and the door was shut behind them.

'Do you mean to say that he opened up the museum specially for us?' asked Serena.

'Yes.' The doctor hailed a taxi and popped her inside and got in beside her. 'There is time for a trip on the canals before lunch,' he told her, and ten minutes later helped her on board one of the excursion boats. There weren't many passengers. Serena sat and gaped and goggled at the lovely old houses lining the canals, rather squashed since the doctor's bulk took up most of the seat. There was a guide on board, explaining everything in three languages, and the doctor sat silent, watching her rapt face, wondering idly how it was that he had thought her a plain girl. The beaky nose was rather charming, and her eyes were really beautiful with their long sweeping lashes. He had no idea why he had had a sudden urge to take her out for the day, and he was already half regretting it. He could have spent the weekend in Friesland with his mother, visited his sisters and brothers, looked up one or two friends, and instead he had elected to spend a day with a mouselike girl who lived a dull life with a selfish mother. However, she wasn't dull and her tongue could be astringent at times. He smiled a little, and Serena, peeping at him, hoped that he wasn't finding it as boring as she had first thought.

They had lunch after the canal tour. They had it in the grill-room, Le Relais: *tomates suisses*, tender steaks with tiny peas and new potatoes, and crème caramel almost hidden in a mound of cream. Serena did justice to all of it, drank the claret she was offered and poured their coffee with a contented sigh. It had been a pleasant meal, she reflected. The doctor, when he chose to be so, could be entertaining, and his manners were excellent. She asked, like a trusting child expecting a treat, 'Where else are we going this afternoon?'

He told her with grave courtesy, 'I thought the Rijksmuseum. It's a must for anyone who comes to Amsterdam.'

'Oh, yes—sixteenth- and seventeenth-century paintings, but aren't there some galleries of porcelain and silver too?'

'Indeed there are. So many tourists go to see the paintings and quite forget the other exhibits. If you are ready we will go.' He glanced at his watch. 'We have the rest of the afternoon.'

Serena walked beside him out into the street again. 'Of course you'll be going out this evening,' she observed composedly, and to his sharp, 'Why do you say that?' she went on, 'Well, you must know any number of people, and because you're Dutch I dare say you have family here as well; you wouldn't want to waste your evening.'

'Are you saying that I am wasting my day?' His voice had an edge to it.

'Good heavens, no, that would be very ill-mannered of me, wouldn't it? I'm having a lovely time and I'm most grateful, but if I were you, I don't think I'd want to take me out.'

'Why not, Serena?' His voice was silky.

'Well, for one thing you've seen all this before, haven't you? And for another, I'm not witty or fascinating or amusing, and I'm nothing much to look at . . .'

'What an abominable girl you are!'

'Am I? I don't mean to be, but we could get on much better together if we just took it for granted that you're you and I'm me.' She gave him an anxious look. 'If you see what I mean?'

He laughed then and stopped in the middle of the pavement and turned her to face him. 'Did I say you were abominable? I'll say it again, for want of a better word.' He turned her round and marched her along until they reached the museum, where they spent over two hours while he explained meticulously the portraits and landscapes, the silver, the porcelain and the glass and furniture.

An early dusk was falling as they left. 'Tea?' he asked as they reached the pavement. 'Dikker and Thijs are fairly close by on the Prinsengracht.' He took her arm and crossed the busy street. 'And let me add that there is plenty of time before my evening date.'

'Then I'd love a cup of tea.'

They had their tea in the elegant surroundings of Dikker and Thijs, and Serena took care not to linger too long over it, something which didn't miss the doctor's sharp eyes, and since it was by now almost dark they took a taxi back to the hotel, waited while the Bentley was driven round from wherever it had been all day, and presently drove back to Mevrouw Blom's house.

The doctor got out with her, thumped the knocker and listened civilly to her thanks, and when Mevrouw Blom opened the door he bade Serena goodnight with casual friendliness and waited politely until she had gone indoors.

'A good day?' asked Mevrouw Blom. 'All are out, for dinner also, but I will get you a fine meal very soon.'

Serena stood in the hall. 'I'm not hungry, Mevrouw Blom. If I could have a sandwich or something presently?'

The kind soul nodded. 'A sandwich, yes, and a bowl of my oh, so good soup, also some coffee. And there is a programme on the *televisie* that you will like. Take off your coat and then come down, eh?'

Serena went to her room. The house was very quiet and the room was chilly. She hung her coat away and put on a pair of soft slippers, and went to look at herself in the small looking-glass.

'I'm surprised he spent the whole day with you, my dear,' she remarked to her reflection. 'He must have been bored. I wonder where he's going this evening? Dinner? Dancing? The theatre? With some lovely creature who can make him laugh...'

She wandered over to the window and looked out at the rooftops around her, feeling lonely, but she didn't stay there long. 'Don't you start being sorry for yourself, my girl!' she said loudly. 'You've had a marvellous day and a heavenly lunch and you've seen a great deal. What more can a girl want?'

She didn't answer her question, but went down-stairs, ate her sandwiches, congratulated Mevrouw Blom on her simply delicious soup and sat down before the TV.

'You are happy?' asked Mevrouw Blom anxiously. 'I have my brother with me, or I would sit with you...'

'I'm fine, Mevrouw Blom. I shall enjoy the tele-vision, and that was a delicious supper.'

So when Mevrouw had gone she was alone, watching a discussion between several clever-looking men, but since they were speaking their own language she couldn't understand what they were saying. It didn't matter, she had a lot to think about; the canals and the lovely old houses lining them, the museum, the hotel and the shops and, of course, the doctor.

Then she glanced at the clock above the stove. He would be dining somewhere by now, and opposite him there would be an elegant, beautifully dressed girl who would call him darling—what was the Dutch for darling? she wondered—and make him laugh. The restaurant, in her mind's eye, would be magnificent with candles on the tables and soft music, and it stood to reason that the food would be superlative. She felt a little sad thinking about it all, especially the doctor.

Marc Dijkstra ter Feulen, eminent medical man, top of his profession and a baron in his own right, was, strangely enough, thinking about Serena. Strangely, because his attention should have been centred on the very pretty woman sitting opposite him. She was nibbling Melba toast while she gave him an amusing account of the trip she had just taken to the South of France. Now if it had been Serena sitting here, he mused, she would have ignored the Melba toast and tucked into the splendid meal without any nonsense about putting on a pound or two. Come to think of it, she was just right as she was. He frowned faintly, remembering that he had expected to have a boring day sightseeing with her, but in fact he had enjoyed himself...

'You may well frown,' said his companion. 'I thought it was disgusting having to wait more than an hour for the plane. I do so dislike tiresome journeys.' She smiled at him. 'Are you going to be here for long, Marc? We haven't seen each other for ages.'

'Another few days at the Hague, and then to Leeuwarden before I go back to London.'

'No days at your home? You work too hard. You need a wife to keep an eye on you.'

He said indifferently, 'I'm far too busy. Would you like to dance?'

Serena went to bed rather early. The clever men had given way to an American film which she remembered seeing a long time ago. Besides, the film had Dutch subtitles which made it all very confusing. She had a shower and washed her hair, then got into bed and went to sleep at once.

It was still quite early when she woke. She peeped into her mother's room and found her sleeping soundly, so she dressed and went quietly downstairs. Mevrouw Blom was setting out cups and saucers for breakfast.

'You sleep well? Good. You want your breakfast? I think no one will come down for a long time, they came home late—one o'clock this morning. Your mother is asleep?'

Serena nodded.

'She goes with Mr Harding to Scheveningen today. He wishes to examine the pier. You will go too?'

'No, I don't think so. I'll see if Mother's awake after I've had breakfast.'

She took as long as possible over her rolls and cheese and coffee, and then went back upstairs. And this time, as she went into her mother's room, Mrs Proudfoot lifted a sleepy head from her pillow.

'Darling, up already? Going somewhere nice, are you? We'll have a nice long chat this evening.'

'Yes, Mother. Have a lovely day.'

Mrs Proudfoot's head sank back on the pillow again and she slept soundly.

The day stretched ahead, and it had to be filled. Church, Serena decided, only which one? She knew at once. The English church in the Begijnhof, of course. There were notices in the hall concerning the times of the various entertainments, the whereabouts of restaurants and museums and when church services were held. She found what she was looking for and decided that if she walked smartly she would be there in time.

'I'll be back for lunch,' she told Mevrouw Blom, and since it was a cold day got into her coat and crammed her one and only hat, a not very becoming felt, on to her head, then hurried out into the street.

There were few people about, and she remembered the way from the drive she had had with the doctor. With minutes to spare she found herself a seat in the little church and sat back, breathing rather hard, for the last few hundred yards had almost been at a trot.

There was quite a large congregation, and presently she looked around her. Mostly elderly people with a sprinkling of children wedged between parents. Her gaze wandered—and came to a surprised halt. Well in front, towering head and shoulders above everyone else, was Dr ter Feulen.

The congregation knelt, and she took the opportunity to peep at him through her fingers. He wouldn't see her, and thank heaven for that; he was most unlikely to turn round and stare about him during the service, and the moment the choir and the vicar had gone out she would nip out.

She stood with everyone else, and while she sang the hymn thanked her stars that she had seen him; to have come face to face with him would have been upsetting, to say the least. He might even think that she was following him around!

She settled down to listen to the sermon, and at the end of it, not having heard a word, sang the last hymn, anxious to be gone. None the less, she couldn't do that before she had breathed a humble little prayer apologising for not giving the service her full attention.

The doctor, casting a keen eye around the church, saw her at once; he was waiting for her as she went out of the church.

Serena walked straight into him and came to an abrupt halt. 'Oh, dear!' she said, and then, 'I had no idea that you would be here,' she told him earnestly.

'Why should you?' He didn't tell her that he had gone to the church on an impulse, guessing that it was the most likely place to find her.

'It's a nice day,' said Serena inanely. 'I'll say goodbye.'

A large hand on her arm stopped her from moving away. 'Coffee? There is a Brown Café here, the coffee is very good. If you intend walking back to Mevrouw Blom's then you must have a drink first.'

She had every intention of refusing, but she was given no chance. He had turned her round and walked her down the *steeg* to the coffee shop, then he sat her down at a small table and ordered coffee before she could think of a graceful refusal.

Over their delicious coffee he asked, 'And what do you intend to do today? An outing with your mother?'

She said too quickly, 'Oh, I expect so. When I left she was only just awake—she was out rather late last night.'

'I dare say she has planned a pleasant afternoon for you. You will be ready to leave, with everything that you might need for a week, for den Haag at eight o'clock tomorrow morning. Don't keep me waiting.'

She eyed him thoughtfully. 'Did Miss Payne ever keep you waiting?'

'Never.'

Greatly daring, she asked, 'And if I do?'

'The question doesn't arise; you won't keep me waiting.' He sounded so absolutely sure of it that she found herself agreeing.

It was pleasant sitting there, but she refused a second cup, thanked him politely and took her leave. He walked with her to the end of the *Steeg*, and watched her walk away.

She walked briskly, wishing to give the impression that she was actually going somewhere, which meant that presently she found herself lost in a tangle of narrow streets leading from the Leidsestraat. Presently she found herself on the Herengracht and turned north instead of south, so that crossing a bridge she found herself in Spuistraat and eventually came out into the Dam Square. It was almost twelve o'clock, and Mevrouw Blom served lunch then. Serena stood uncertainly, not quite sure which way to go. The sight of a taxi solved her problem. She waved it down, gave the address in her carefully learned Dutch and was whisked back just in time.

'I am full of worry,' observed Mevrouw Blom. 'I think that perhaps you are lost.'

'Well, I was just for a bit. I hope I haven't kept everyone waiting.'

'No, no, they are all gone until the evening—to Schevingenen. I have soup for you, and cheese and cold meat.'

'I'm sorry you had to get lunch just for me, Mevrouw Blom. I could easily have had a sandwich out.'

'I must eat also, it is no trouble. But this afternoon? You go out again?'

'Well, no. I have to go to den Haag in the morning and I must pack a few things.'

'You will not mind if I go to my sister's? It is a good chance, with so few guests...'

'Of course not.'

'I will leave tea if you would not mind to boil the water?'

'Of course not.' A quiet afternoon, Serena told herself, was just what she would like.

It was certainly quiet once Mevrouw Blom had gone. She packed her case, made sure that she had a notebook, pencils and pen ready to use and went downstairs to the sitting-room, switched on the TV and went to make herself a cup of tea. The kitchen was cosy and rather old-fashioned. She lingered as long as possible and then bore the tea-tray back and sat down by the stove to drink her tea, leaf through some Dutch magazines and glance from time to time at the television, also Dutch. The hours passed slowly and she was glad when she heard Mevrouw Blom's key in the lock. But it was another two hours before her mother and Mr Harding came in.

'There you are, darling!' exclaimed Mrs Proudfoot. 'Have you had a lovely day? I haven't enjoyed myself so much for years... Now I'm exhausted. Be an angel and take my things upstairs and bring me back my other shoes—the black pumps.'

She sat down in the chair Serena had vacated and patted the sofa close to it. 'Come and sit by me,' she begged Mr Harding prettily, 'and tell me some more about the King of Prussia, William the First, arriving there at the end of the wars with Napoleon.'

It was some time before Serena had the chance to tell her mother that she would be going to den Haag in the morning.

'The Hague? But, darling, why? I know the doctor was going to work there, but surely you could go to and fro each day?'

'It's about fifty miles, Mother, and it's only for a week.'

Her mother pouted. 'And am I not allowed to see something of it?'

Serena was saved from answering by Mr Harding. 'Margaret, I promise you you'll miss nothing—I shall be going there in a few days' time to study the architecture of the Ridderzaal, and I shall be delighted if you would accompany me each day.'

Mrs Proudfoot smiled. 'Well, in that case, Arthur, I'll say no more. Indeed, I shall enjoy a visit there so much more with someone who can explain everything to me.' She gave him an arch look. 'I'm not much good on my own, you know, I've always lived such a sheltered life.'

Serena gave a small sigh of relief, and at the same time stifled a feeling of hurt because her mother had forgotten to ask her what she had done with her day.

Not that it mattered. Except for half an hour in Dr ter Feulen's unpredictable company, the day had been extremely dull.

She was ready when the doctor arrived in the morning. She had bidden her mother goodbye, assuring her that she would be back by the start of the following week and promising to phone in the evening. She got into the Bentley, waved goodbye to Mevrouw Blom and sat as quiet as a mouse as Dr ter Feulen wove his way through the early morning traffic and out on to the road to den Haag.

Once they were clear of the city he said, 'I have an outpatients' clinic this morning, and I shall want to have you there to take notes. This afternoon I have a number of consultations. I should like the notes typed up by five o'clock—there won't be very many. Someone will bring you a folder during the afternoon—the book I am writing. Type as much as you can before you leave the hospital.'

'And when will that be?' asked Serena.

'Six o'clock or thereabouts,' he told her carelessly. 'Tomorrow I shall be in theatre, anaesthetising. Carry on with the manuscript until I send you my letters.'

'Very well. Where am I to lodge?'

'In the nurses' home—it is a few yards from the hospital. There is a canteen there where you will get your meals. You have no need to worry or pay for anything—that is all taken care of. The following day I shall be at a children's hospital, and you will go with me.'

Serena said faintly, 'You're going to be busy.'

'So are you, make no mistake about that.' He glanced at her. 'Too much for you?' he wanted to know blandly.

'Certainly not! If Miss Payne coped I suppose I can too.'

He said casually, 'Oh, Muriel took everything in her stride; she was most competent.'

'I'm not sure if that's meant to encourage me or warn me to expect the sack,' said Serena tartly.

He laughed then. 'Neither. Believe me, Serena, you would have been back in England by now if you hadn't measured up to her standards. You'll do very well.'

'I'm flattered.'

'I never flatter.'

His profile looked so stern that she forbore from saying another word.

The hospital in den Haag was large and modern. On their arrival Serena was whisked away by a severe woman in an old-fashioned nurse's uniform and a fiercely starched cap with its tail hanging down her back.

'You will come with me,' said this lady in a voice that dared her to disagree, then she led the way, away from the doctor, who muttered a casual,

'I'll see you presently, Serena.'

Serena was walked briskly along a number of corridors, taken up several floors in a lift and led through a swing-door into a corridor very like the one in Amsterdam. 'Your office,' said her companion. 'Leave your things here. There is a cloakroom at the end of the corridor where you may tidy yourself.' Her look implied that this was an urgent necessity. 'You will take your midday meal at noon and someone will come for you and show you where to go.'

'My room?' asked Serena, getting a word in edgeways.

'After your midday meal you will be shown your room. Your case will be taken there in the meantime.' The severe lady eyed her doubtfully. 'I hope you will be happy during your stay.'

'Oh, so do I,' said Serena fervently, but not quite sure about it.

CHAPTER FOUR

SERENA barely had time to tidy herself, arrange her desk to her liking and put her notebook and pen ready before the phone on her desk rang.

'Take the lift,' said the doctor's voice in her ear, 'and come down to the ground floor. Someone will meet you there.' He hung up before she could say a word.

She got into the lift and was met by a solemn young man in large glasses. 'Miss Proudfoot?' He offered a hand. 'Dirk Moerman.'

They shook hands rather solemnly, but he gave her no time to speak. 'This way,' he urged her, and hurried her along another corridor and into a vast hall overflowing with people sitting on long benches and all talking animatedly. There was a young woman with a trolley serving coffee, and Serena's little beaky nose twitched at its aroma. A smell of it was all she was likely to get if even a fraction of the people there were outpatients of the doctor's!

His consulting-room was at the other end of the hall and he was already at his desk, reading the notes being handed to him by a tall, very pretty girl in a sister's uniform. She looked up and smiled at Serena, but Dr ter Feulen merely twitched an eyebrow. 'That chair over there in the corner, Serena.' Then, to her surprise, 'Have you had your coffee?'

She sat composedly. 'No, sir.'

He waved a hand at the sister, who in turn said something to a nurse who had just joined them. Then he said, 'You had better gulp it down now, you won't have another chance. This is Zuster de Vries, she speaks very good English.'

Serena nodded and smiled and longed suddenly to speak very good Dutch. She drank the coffee when it was brought, trying to make sense of what was being said around her. No wonder they all spoke English so well, for no one but the Dutch could understand their own language, although presently she was cheered to hear several medical terms which sounded near enough to those in English. She polished off the coffee, tucked back a stray wisp of mousy hair and held her pencil at the ready as a very stout lady was ushered in. She looked frightened, and Serena watched the doctor put her at her ease before starting his patient questioning. He had charm, she reflected as she took down his concise notes, taking care to get the medical terms right. He might be quite nice... His calm voice stopped and he spoke to the sister, who led the patient away to a cubicle. He talked for a few minutes to the youngish man who had just joined him and turned to Serena.

'This is my registrar, Willem Bakker—Serena Proudfoot—I mentioned her. Add this to my notes, if you please...' He dictated for a few moments and when he had finished Serena said softly,

'Oh, the poor soul!'

'Fortunately it's curable. We'll have her in at once, Willem.'

He went away to examine his patient then and Willem Bakker with him. Presently, from the agitated voice from the cubicle, Serena guessed that the patient had been told that she would need surgery. At intervals, between the cries and outbursts of the woman, she could hear the doctor being soothing—to good effect, for presently they all emerged once again and the patient was led away looking quite cheerful.

Dr ter Feulen sat himself down again, spoke to the sister and buried his nose in the papers before him, but he got to his feet as the next patient was ushered in—an old man, bone-thin, well turned out in well-worn clothes, with bright blue eyes in a calm face.

He wished everyone good day and sat down and said something to the doctor to make him laugh a little. The pair of them talked for a minute or two, and then went into the little cubicle, but not for long. The old man came out with the doctor, still spruce and cheerful, bade everyone goodbye and went away. The doctor sat down again.

'Lucius de Groot,' he began to dictate. 'Carcinoma of left lung. Refuses admission. Non-operable. Reference notes...' He quoted numbers. 'A delightful man,' he added to Serena.

The morning wore on, but no one looked at the clock. The doctor was apparently tireless and expected everyone else to be the same. From time to time the nurse would appear briefly, whisper to Sister and go again, and it wasn't until almost two o'clock that the last patient for the doctor's clinic went away.

The doctor got to his feet, thanked everyone with cool politeness and went away with his registrar. Zuster de Vries smiled at Serena. 'A long morning—you know where to go to eat?' When Serena shook her head she said, 'Then you come with me.' She glanced at her watch. 'I have only a short time before the next clinic. But I eat first.'

The canteen was at the back of the hospital, a large
airy place with a long counter running its length and
tables set in orderly rows. Very like the hospital at
home, reflected Serena, collecting a tray and joining
Zuster de Vries to assemble soup, cheese rolls, a salad
and coffee on it. While they ate, sitting alone in the
empty room, they talked.

The Dutch girl was friendly. 'I will tell Zuster Graaf
to come here and show you to your room. You will
work this afternoon?'

'Oh, yes. Dr ter Feulen wants the notes by five
o'clock and then I'm to type up his manuscript.'

Zuster de Vries nodded her pretty head. 'He works
hard, so we work hard also.'

'He's not always here? I mean, what do you do
when he's away?'

The other girl rolled her eyes. 'Work—Willem
Bakker sees to that—and the doctor comes many
times, sometimes just for a day, perhaps two, to
operate or examine some difficult cases. He also goes
to Amsterdam—but you know that.'

Serena finished her coffee. 'Yes, he works hard in
London too.'

'He is a good man, but—how do you say?—
wrapped in himself?'

The pair of them left the canteen, and Zuster de
Vries went to a wall phone and talked for a few moments. 'She comes, Zuster Graaf. You will wait here?
I must go back now.' She smiled dazzlingly. 'Tomorrow it is my free day and I go with my fiancé to
his home.'

'I hope you have a lovely time.' Serena was aware
of a distinct feeling of relief at the news, although she
didn't know why.

Zuster de Vries paused in her flight. 'You have a boyfriend? You are engaged?'

Serena shook her head and gave what she hoped was a carefree smile.

'You should have—you are a nice girl. Dr ter Feulen told me so.'

Serena was left pondering this remark, trying to make something of it and failing. Not for long, however, for the severe woman arrived, looking a shade less severe, thank heaven. 'You come with me?' she invited, and looked pleased when Serena said,

'Thank you, Zuster Graaf.'

The nurses' home was in a ten-storey block built on to the hospital and reached by an outside passage or a bridge on its fourth floor. Serena's room was on this floor and close to the bridge—something, painstakingly pointed out by Zuster Graaf, that would make it easier for Serena to get herself to and from the hospital.

Serena thanked her gratefully and admired her room. It was small but comfortable, with bright curtains at its window and a warm bedspread on the divan bed. The shower-rooms were at the end of the corridor, she was told, and she would be called each morning with the nurses at half-past six. 'You are expected to have your light out by half-past eleven,' concluded Zuster Graaf.

If the morning's work was anything to go by, thought Serena, her light would be out long before then.

Left to herself, she unpacked her few things and sped back to the room where she was to work. By dint of keeping strictly to the task at hand she had the notes ready by five o'clock, and, since no one had told her how long she was to work, she started on the doctor's manuscript.

It was an involved work full of incomprehensible words and couched in the sort of language she supposed members of the medical profession understood. Probably the work of a genius written in almost unintelligible script. She hoped she was getting it right.

It was almost six o'clock and she was tired, hungry and thirsty. No one had come near her since a mug of tea had been offered round about three o'clock, and she had neglected to ask at what time she was supposed to stop work and, what was more important, when she might eat her supper.

She looked up hopefully as the door opened, but it was Dr ter Feulen, a sheaf of papers in one hand, and her face fell.

'Not pleased to see me?' he wanted to know blandly.

'I'm pleased to see anyone,' she told him tartly. 'I should like to know for how long I go on working and where and when there'll be any supper?' She added crossly, 'And now you're here, with more work!'

'No, no,' he told her soothingly, 'merely work for tomorrow. I am sorry if no one told you about working hours and meals. You work until six o'clock and go to the canteen for your supper at half-past seven. You don't need to go if you wish to spend your evening elsewhere. I thought that perhaps we might have dinner together?'

'Us? Have dinner?' Her surprise hardly flattered him, and the corners of his firm mouth twitched with amusement.

'Well, we have to eat, do we not? And I for one am hungry—and I must add that I have a busy day tomorrow and there will be no time in which to tell you what I shall want you to do.'

'Oh, well, in that case,' she conceded kindly, and added, 'I haven't anything to wear...'

'Somewhere quiet,' he assured her. 'I'll be outside in the car in fifteen minutes.'

He held the door open for her and she skipped past him, her mind already intent on what she should wear.

It was clear it would have to be the green jersey. She raced through a shower and got into it, did her face and hair and pushed her feet into the plain black pumps she so seldom wore. Her reflection in the long looking-glass in the corridor wasn't encouraging. The dress was all right, it fitted her and it had a certain elegance; all the same, it was the kind of dress no one ever saw... She put on the jacket, found a handbag and raced back to the hospital and out of its front door, to skid to a halt within inches of the doctor's substantial bulk.

He greeted her with one hand. 'I would have waited, you know,' he told her gently. 'With four sisters I have been educated to expect all women to be at least fifteen minutes later than the time arranged.'

'Four sisters?' Serena stood on the pavement looking up at him in surprise. Somehow she had never considered the possibility of his having a family—parents, brothers, sisters... 'Brothers too?'

'Three.'

'Well, I never!' She stared up at him with her lovely hazel eyes, fringed with their long curling lashes. 'What I mean is... well...'

She paused, and he helped her out with smiling ease. 'I'm the eldest.' He smiled down at her and opened the car door. 'I hope you're hungry—I had to miss lunch.'

She had barely glimpsed den Haag that morning; it was dark now and she had no idea where they were going. He drove through the centre of the city and within a few minutes turned into a broad street leading away from its heart. 'There's a very pleasant place in Wassenaar—that's the outskirts of den Haag. We're almost there.' He glanced sideways at her quiet face. 'I expect you're tired—I've worked you hard.'

'You warned me,' she reminded him, 'and it was all very interesting. I wish I understood more about your work, but I dare say I'll pick up the basic facts in time.'

He had turned into a narrow tree-lined street and parked the car beside what appeared to be a country inn—a sight to reassure Serena, still doubtful about the green jersey. Inside, she felt even better, for it was in truth an inn, decked out with little tables with coloured tablecloths, candlelit, and with a heavily beamed low ceiling. There was a bar at one end and a fair number of people, some of them dressed as simply as she was. She heaved a sigh of relief, not unnoticed by her companion, and surrendered her jacket before being led to the bar.

They drank their sherry and studied the menu. It might be a country inn, Serena reflected, but a very expensive one, judging by the prices, which even when changed into pounds were sky-high. With an eye on the doctor's pocket she selected the lowest-priced food she could find, only to have her choice quietly contradicted. 'Take my advice,' he begged her, 'the garlic mushrooms are delicious and they do a splendid lobster here. May I alter your mind for you?'

He didn't wait for her answer but spoke to the waiter, ordered wine without looking at the wine list and settled back in his chair. 'What do you think of the hospital?' he wanted to know. His quiet, friendly manner invited confidence, and Serena, long starved of a sympathetic listener, for her mother had no interest in hospitals or indeed anything that smacked of illness, gave her opinions full rein.

The doctor listened gravely, putting in an encouraging word here and there, and if he was amused at some of her remarks nothing, save a gleam in his half-shut eyes, showed of it.

They dined presently at a table set discreetly in a window where they could observe without being observed. Serena looked around her with pleasure, happily unaware that he had asked for a table where the plainness of her dress would go largely unobserved. His discerning eye had seen quickly enough that while at first sight the women there appeared to be simply dressed, the simplicity was expensive, and for some reason he hadn't bothered to probe he didn't want Serena to feel unhappy about that.

He was a practised host and a pleasant companion when he chose to be. She ate the mushrooms and the lobster and on his advice followed them by a mountainous confection of ice-cream, chocolate and whipped cream topped off thickly with nuts and candied fruit. She drank the wine he poured for her, but refused a second glass, nor would she have brandy with her coffee. 'I'm not very used to it,' she told him matter-of-factly. 'I don't go out a great deal.'

Hardly ever, but she wasn't going to tell him that. She had refilled his coffee-cup when he said, 'I should like you to go on with the manuscript tomorrow. You will most likely not get my letters until the late afternoon. I should like them ready to sign by half-past six at the latest; I've an evening engagement . . .' He went on to detail the rest of the week: clinics, a session with private patients which she would attend, two more theatre sessions the notes of which would have to be typed up, and more clinics. 'You will be free on Saturday and Sunday. Be ready to return to Amsterdam with me on Monday morning. I'll give you the time later on in the week.'

Serena observed that their pleasant evening was over, a matter for regret on her part but perhaps not on his. It had been delightful; she told him in her sensible way that she would like to return to the hospital, 'For I've plenty of work waiting for me in the morning, and you will have too. Thank you very much for my delicious dinner, and in such a de-lightful place . . .' She looked round her once more and this time took note of the women's clothes. 'I'm not dressed for it, you know—you don't mind?'

She spoke with the unconscious candour of a child and without self-pity, and the doctor said kindly, 'You look very nice, Serena, and I wouldn't have minded if you were wearing a potato sack.' Which wasn't quite true, but with four sisters to practise on he had per-fected the art of saying the right thing and at the right time.

He was rewarded by the pleased smile on her face. Oh, good.'

At the hospital he got out, opened the car door and was at her side to show her in to the entrance hall. He wished her a pleasant but brief goodnight and went along one of the downstairs corridors. From his pur-poseful walk Serena concluded that he had already forgotten her. Why should he remember me? she reflected, making her way over to the nurses' home and her room.

She didn't see him the next day. She typed his manuscript, wished she could understand even a small part of it, and soon after four o'clock a porter brought her a pile of letters as well as notes from the doctor's day in theatre. She abandoned the manuscript with relief, dealt with the letters and started on the notes. It was almost half-past six by then, and when the same porter came back she gave him the letters, tidied her desk and went over to the nurses' home. Supper and an hour watching the TV in the company of some of the other nurses in the nicely furnished sitting-room filled the rest of the evening, and she went to bed armed with a Dutch-English dictionary one of the nurses had lent her. It had some useful phrases tucked away on the back page. She tried out those under the heading 'Restaurants and dining'; it was most unlikely that the doctor would ever ask her out again, but one never knew... She had got as far as 'Toast, buttered or dry' when she fell asleep.

The rest of the week went by in a punishing round of constant work. By Friday evening Serena was heartily sick of her little office, and had she had the strength she would gladly have hurled the typewriter through the window, but she had coped with everything, obeying the doctor's terse instructions to the letter, never looking at the clock, mindful of Miss Payne's perfections. To her surprise he had put his head round the door as she was tidying everything away for the last time and thanked her for her hard work. 'I'll take those if they're ready,' he said, and scooped up the papers and letters she had just finished. 'Be outside by eight o'clock on Monday morning. We will go straight to the hospital from here, but after the morning clinic I shan't need you until the following morning, so you will be able to go to Mevrouw Blom's and see your mother.'

She thanked him and watched him walk away down the corridor before switching off the lights and closing the doors, vexed that she had forgotten to thank him for the envelope she had found on her desk that morning. There were Dutch banknotes in it and his scrawled message that she might like some of her salary so that she could shop if she wished.

It was delightful to have a whole day to herself. She had telephoned her mother on the previous evening, but she had been out and Mevrouw Blom had told her that she and Mr Harding were planning to go to Arnhem at the weekend and should she give her a message. Serena had told her not to bother. 'Just say that I'll be back some time on Monday, please, Mevrouw Blom, and give her my love.'

She had rung off feeling let down; there had been the vague idea that her mother might have come to den Haag for the day and they could have gone shopping together, but probably Arnhem would be much more interesting.

She went out soon after breakfast with a map and a guidebook and spent the morning inspecting the Ridderzaal, then she took herself through the Binnenhof to the Mauritshuis, a lovely Dutch Renaissance house, its rooms filled with the finest seventeenth-century paintings. She could have stayed there for a very long time, but she had a lot to see still, so she went along Korte Vijverberg and Lange

Vijverberg so that she could admire the façades of the old houses there. By then she was hungry and went in search of a coffee house, where she ate a *kaas broodje* and drank several cups of coffee before setting off once more. The shops, she decided, as she had Sunday in which to explore the churches and the parks, so the afternoon was spent with her small nose pressed to boutique windows, showcases of jewellery and small shops filled with expensive leather goods. She turned away from them finally and went into the Bijenkorf, which had the familiarity of a small Selfridges, had an elegant tea on the balcony high above the busy counters below and then went in search of a present for her mother and something for Mevrouw Blom; silver filigree earrings for her mother and a silk headscarf for Mevrouw Blom, who never seemed to leave the house without one. She browsed round the delightful cosmetic counters too, and after a good deal of deliberation bought a new lipstick and a cream guaranteed to erase lines and wrinkles. That she had neither was a small matter; she was fulfilling an urge to improve her looks.

She spent Sunday exploring den Haag once again, the churches this time; Sint Jacobs Kerk, and close by the Holy Ghost Almshouses, hardly changed in three hundred years. From there she walked to the Kloosterkerk and presently found a coffee shop for her snack lunch, and since it was a cold day she had a bowl of *erwtensoep*, almost solid with peas and tiny pieces of ham and sausage.

Madurodam was something she had promised herself she would see. Armed with the number of the tram she must take in order to reach it, she paid her modest bill and went back into the street.

It was as wonderful as the nurses in the hospital had told her—a miniature city; streets, already lighted since the afternoon was dimming to dusk, canals, trains, trams and buses, houses of every description, churches, theatres and shops. There was even an airport and an amusement park. She spent a long time there, until the chilly evening reminded her that she needed some tea. She took a tram back to the centre of den Haag, had tea in an elegant and wickedly expensive café, then went back to the hospital. A lovely weekend, she decided, as she went to her room. She felt vaguely guilty about it, for of course the doctor would have been hard at work.

Nothing of the sort. He had spent a delightful weekend in Friesland.

Serena was punctual on Monday morning, but he was already waiting in the car. He got out, put her case in the boot and opened the door for her.

'I'm not late——' she began.

'Good morning, Serena. No, I am early, so smooth your ruffled feathers and tell me what you did with your weekend.'

He was at his most amiable, and she responded happily, but was careful to keep her remarks brief in case he got bored. They were approaching Amsterdam in a welter of early morning traffic when he observed, 'I have to spend a few days in Leeuwarden in Friesland—a couple of lectures and some consultations. From there we shall return to England. You will go with me—it will be a good opportunity to get on with the manuscript.'

She said quietly, 'Yes, Doctor,' and then, 'My mother?'

'I imagine she will be agreeable to remaining in Amsterdam for another few days? We can pick her up on our way back.' He gave her a brief glance. 'You can discuss it with her this afternoon.'

'Yes. When do you wish to go to Friesland?'

'Let me see, today is Monday. I have a list there on Friday morning, so we should drive up there on Thursday evening. They will put you up in the nurses' home there. If there are no hindrances, we should leave there on the following Monday. You will be back home some time that day. I'm sorry I can't be more explicit at the moment.'

They were silent then until he stopped the car before the hospital entrance, got out to open the door for her, fetched her case and carried it as far as the lift.

'I'll see you in about twenty minutes,' he told her, 'in the outpatients' clinic.'

There were a great many patients. Serena filled her notebook and hoped that the doctor wouldn't want everything typed by five o'clock. It seemed that he didn't. The clinic over at last, he told her, 'Go to Mevrouw Blom's after your lunch. There is no need for you to come back until nine o'clock tomorrow, —type what you can. I shall be operating tomorrow, so you will have the morning in which to finish them. There will be letters in the afternoon.' At the door he turned to say, 'Take a taxi and add it to your expenses.'

Serena went back to her office, put everything ready to start work later on, hurried down to the canteen for a quick meal and, dressed and with her nightcase in her hand, got a taxi and was ringing Mevrouw Blom's doorbell in nice time for the afternoon cup of tea.

Mevrouw Blom prided herself on adapting her ways to her guests. The English liked their tea at four o'clock, so that was when it was served. She was coming into the hall with her empty tea-tray when Serena rang the bell, and she opened the door at once. Her welcome was warm.

'Serena, just as I take in the teapot! Take off your jacket and go at once to the drawing-room. Your case can stay in the hall.' She beamed in her kindly fashion. 'You tell me all soon, eh?'

Serena said that yes, of course she would, and went into the drawing-room. They were all there, and there were cries of, 'Well, well, Serena, how nice!' and, 'Just in time for tea,' and, 'Are you staying?'

She smiled and murmured replies, then went to her mother to kiss her. 'Darling!' cried Mrs Proudfoot. 'How simply lovely to see you!' She studied her daughter's face. 'You look very tired, you should do something about your hair—have it tinted. Have you had a lovely time? Met lots of new friends and gone on the town?' She patted the chair beside her. 'Come and sit down beside me.' Someone handed Serena a cup of tea and her mother went on, 'I've had such a splendid week! We—that is, Mr Harding and I—have been to so many places I've lost count.' She gave a pretty little laugh. 'Silly little me, but it was all so interesting.'

There was a general babble of talk, with Mijnheer van Til airing his English at some length and Mijnheer Lagerveld, not to be outdone, enthusing about the delights of den Haag, their wives nodding and smiling as though they understood every word. Mr Harding had very little to say, though.

Tea over, Mrs Proudfoot excused herself charmingly. 'I must go upstairs with Serena,' she apologised smilingly, 'and help her unpack!'

Something she had never done in her life before. Serena supposed it was an excuse to have a chat, and she was glad of the chance to tell her mother that she was off to Friesland in a few days. She didn't think her mother would mind; she seemed very happy at Mevrouw Blom's.

In her room she opened her case and started to take out her things, while her mother strolled over to the window and stared out into the street below.

'Mother,' began Serena carefully, 'I quite thought we would be going back to London this week, but the doctor has to go to Leeuwarden and I'm to go with him. Would you mind staying here for just a few more days?'

Her mother turned round, laughing. 'But my dear girl, nothing could be better! Mr Harding is returning to England on Wednesday and has offered me a lift, and I've accepted. You know how I hate flying. We shall go in his car and I shan't have to bother about anything.' She saw the look on Serena's face and added, 'Besides, it really is time I went back to the house and made sure that everything is all right. It has been lovely here, darling, but this is too good a chance to miss, travelling from door to door in comfort.'

Serena said, 'Yes, of course, Mother. You'll be all right on your own at the house?' She folded a blouse slowly. 'I shall be back in a week, I suppose—Dr ter Feulen didn't say exactly when.'

'I shall be perfectly OK,' said her mother sharply. 'I'm not an old woman, you know, Serena!' She glanced in the looking-glass and patted her hair. 'Of course you must stay, since you work for the doctor. You must be having a lovely time.'

'Yes, Mother. I'd better tell Dr ter Feulen, hadn't I?'

Mrs Proudfoot frowned. 'Why bother? It must be all the same to him whether I go or stay. Tell him on Wednesday—better still, I'll write him a little note and you can give it to him.'

'Very well. I'm sorry we haven't had the chance to go anywhere together. It would have been fun to have done some shopping.'

'Oh, darling, that reminds me—I bought the prettiest dress in Arnhem. There are some lovely shops there. Very pale grey crêpe with the most elegant cut— you must see it.' With that Mrs Proudfoot went to the door. 'I'll leave you to get tidy, darling—see you at dinner.' She paused at the door to ask, 'You're staying here?'

'Only for this afternoon, Mother. I'm going back to work tomorrow on an early morning bus. Dr ter Feulen thought I'd like to see how you were.'

Her mother made a little face. 'Then I'd better write that note and let you have it this evening and we can say goodbye then, my pet. You know how awful I feel if I don't get my sleep, and I'll be out tomorrow night.'

When she had gone Serena sat down on her bed. She would have liked a good cry, but there was neither the time nor the place. Besides, she should be feeling delighted that her mother was so happy after her years of ill health. However, she wasn't delighted. She was hurt and lonely and forlorn, and unless she snapped out of it she would be wallowing in self-pity. She finished her unpacking; after their evening meal she would have to do some washing. The doctor hadn't said if they were to go to Friesland from the hospital or whether she would have an hour or two at Mevrouw Blom's. She would have to ask.

She did her face and her hair, changed into another blouse and went downstairs again.

She would have to be up early the next morning, but since Mevrouw Blom was an early riser that was no problem. She said goodbye to her mother, took the letter for the doctor and, after due thought, re-packed her case. For all she knew he would want to go straight to Friesland from the hospital on Thursday. She wondered idly as she did so who saw to his spotless linen and his beautifully pressed suits; he never looked anything but immaculate.

She was at her desk by nine o'clock, eyeing the little pile of letters and notes already on it. The manuscript was there too. She set to work and typed steadily until her lunch break. When she got back there was another pile, notes of the work he had been doing in theatre all the morning. She had them ready by half-past five and had embarked on the manuscript once more when he walked in.

His nod was casual. 'I'll sign everything here—perhaps you would take them down to the lodge as you go.'

Her, 'Yes, sir,' was, as usual, quiet.

'Your mother is well?' His head was bent over his papers.

'Yes, thank you. I—that is, she asked me to give you this note.'

He put out a hand, not looking at her, finished what he was doing and opened it. Serena watched his face as he read. It was impossible to know what he was thinking from its blandness.

'You have no objection to staying on for a few more days?' he wanted to know. 'Your mother seems quite content with her plans.'

'Of course I'll stay,' she told him matter-of-factly. 'Mother came because you were kind enough to allow her to do so. I'm very grateful; she's been very happy...'

'And no longer suffering ill health,' he added drily. 'I'm glad.'

He picked up his pen again and finished signing the papers. 'I must go—I'm already rather late. What do you do with your evenings, Serena?'

She was taken by surprise. 'Well, there's supper and the TV, and I'm trying to learn one or two Dutch phrases...' It sounded pretty thin.

She watched him go after wishing her goodnight and giving her a brief reminder that, since he would be operating again in the morning, she was to get on with the book.

The days passed quickly. Serena phoned her mother on Wednesday morning and wished her a good trip home. 'I'll ring you this evening,' she told her. 'You'll be back by then.'

'No, don't do that, darling,' said Mrs Proudfoot hastily. 'I shall be exhausted after such a long journey, even in comfort, so I shall go straight to bed. Give me your phone number and I'll ring you.'

'I'm going to Friesland on Thursday,' Serena reminded her.

'Oh, I'll get in touch during the morning, darling. Have fun!' Her mother had rung off.

There was a final clinic on Thursday morning, and it seemed to Serena that there were more patients than ever. They were to leave at six o'clock from the hospital, and she had found time to phone Mevrouw Blom to tell her so. It was early afternoon before her mother telephoned, to say that she had had a delightful journey and she intended to spend a few days quietly. 'And see you very shortly, darling,' she added airily, 'and mind you have some fun!'

Serena cast a rather jaundiced eye at the pile of notes still waiting to be typed. They hardly allowed for fun, and she supposed it would be the same in Friesland and indeed in London once they returned.

She reminded herself that she had no reason to complain. Her salary was good, she had a pleasant home to go to each evening and her mother's company. She finished her work and wasted a few minutes doing sums on a piece of typing paper. She would have more than enough to buy all the clothes she wanted and contribute more to the household budget too. She covered the typewriter, left her desk neat and hurried to get ready to leave with the doctor.

CHAPTER FIVE

'Have you had a meal?' the doctor asked her as he urged her into the car and took her case.

Serena hadn't had the time, but she wasn't going to say so. Her, 'Yes, thank you,' was prim.

'A pity. I didn't stop for lunch and the cup of tea Theatre Sister gave me did no more than whet my appetite.'

He got in beside her and fastened his seatbelt. He sounded resigned, and her warm heart was touched. 'As a matter of fact,' she told him, 'I haven't had anything since lunch.' And when he turned his cold questioning eye on her, 'Yes, I know, but I didn't want . . . that is, I thought you were being polite—you know what I mean?'

'No, I don't know what you mean, and I am never polite unless the occasion merits it. Serena, don't fib to me again.'

'Well, I won't unless I really need to.'

'That need should not arise. There is a place in Hoorn, we can get there in half an hour.'

He started the car and, once free of Amsterdam, drove north. The restaurant in Hoorn was pleasant, brightly lighted and only half full. They had a table in the window and ate *sole bonne femme*, braised celery and plain boiled potatoes, and, since the doctor was driving and Serena liked it, they drank Vichy water and followed that with *poffertjes* and coffee, and while they ate he outlined his programme for the next two days. 'I shall be in theatre all day tomorrow, and on Saturday there are one or two cases lined up for me. I'm on the hospital board and there will be a meeting some time during the day. There will be the notes of the theatre cases for you to type and file, the rest of the time you can get on with the book.'

'Will you be working on Sunday?' she asked.

'No. We shall leave on Monday morning. I'll tell you when later on.'

It was dark by now. They left the restaurant and drove on, over the Afsluitdijk and into Friesland, and since it was impossible to see any of the scenery the doctor didn't bother to tell Serena anything about it, leaving her to peer through her window as they swept through one small village after another. Only as they slowed to go through a sizeable town did he say, 'Franeker—we're almost there.'

'The signposts aren't in Dutch,' said Serena. 'Or some of them aren't.'

'Well, of course not, we're in Friesland now, and everyone speaks Fries.'

'Not Dutch as well?'

'Of course they speak Dutch, but among themselves they speak their own language.'

'Oh—do they speak English? I've managed to learn one or two basic sentences in Dutch...'

'Have you, indeed? But don't worry, English is widely spoken.'

He was slowing the car again as they entered Leeuwarden, driving down a broad road lined with fair-sized red brick houses. They could have been in the outskirts of Bath or Basingstoke. But the houses faded away, and the road became narrow as they reached the heart of the city. The streets were almost empty by now, but the shop windows were lighted and Serena could see that the buildings were old and picturesque, but she had very little time to look. The doctor swept the car into a narrow street and turned in between two stone pillars, into a courtyard beyond which she could see the hospital. It was large, larger than she had expected, and from what she could see modern, its lighted windows giving it a cheerful appearance.

The doctor undid her seatbelt and got out to open her door, and she waited quietly while he got her case from the boot, then followed him to the entrance. There was a porter there. He held open the door and, when the doctor spoke to him, took her case and nodded before going to the lodge to telephone.

'You weren't speaking Dutch,' observed Serena.

'Of course not.' The doctor smiled down at her in what she considered to be a rather smug fashion. 'I'm Friesian.'

He turned away to take the phone from the porter and presently put it down and came back to her. 'HoofdZuster Grimstra is coming for you. She will take you to your room and you will be called in the morning, shown where to have your meals and then taken to the room where you are to work. If you get into difficulties, you can contact me.'

'But I won't know where you are.' Serena suddenly felt lonely.

'No, but anyone here will know how to reach me.' He said something to the porter, who listened and then nodded. 'Piet here will tell the porters on duty to keep an eye on you. If you want me—but only if it's urgent, please—it will be enough for you to say my name to one of them.'

She wondered what it must be like to be so important that everyone knew immediately who you were. She thanked him, and he smiled, but not at her. She turned round to face the person who had just joined them—a splendidly built woman, not young but handsome, with fine blue eyes and grey hair pinned into an old-fashioned bun. She wore uniform and an imposing cap and held herself very erect.

She shook the doctor's hand and smiled at him, exchanging a few words before he said, 'This is Serena Proudfoot, my secretary. HoofdZuster Grimstra, who will look after you. Go with her now, Serena.' He saw her slight frown and added, 'If you please. I'll see you some time tomorrow.'

Her, 'Goodnight, sir,' was uttered in a waspish voice.

She had to trot to keep up with HoofdZuster Grimstra's stride. They went through the long corridor running from one end of the hospital to the other and climbed the stairs leading from a second entrance hall.

'This door you will use,' said her companion, 'also this staircase. The nurses' home is through this door.'

They had reached a wide landing and she opened a stout door on one side of it. Another long corridor, lined with doors, one of which she opened and ushered Serena inside. The room was very like those she had slept in at the other hospitals, with a welcome addition.

'You like tea,' stated HoofdZuster Grimstra, 'therefore here is a tray and a kettle and a teapot.'

'How very kind!' Serena smiled happily at her. 'Thank you very much.'

'You will be called at seven o'clock, a nurse will show you to the dining-room. I wish you a good night, Serena.'

HoofdZuster Grimstra nodded and smiled and made her stately way back along the corridor, leaving Serena to examine her room. There were tea-bags, little packets of powdered milk and sugar lumps arranged neatly on a tray beside the kettle. She took off her jacket, filled the kettle from the washbasin and switched it on, reflecting that the Dutch sister was both kind and thoughtful for her comfort. In this she was correct; she didn't know that the dear soul was only obeying the doctor's request, indeed it would have been the last thing that she would have expected of him.

A cheerful young nurse came for her in the morning and bore her down to the ground floor for her breakfast, and when she had eaten her bread and butter and cheese and drunk the delicious coffee, HoofdZuster Grimstra carried her off to a small room high up in the hospital where she found the doctor's manuscript on a desk beside a typewriter and enough paper to keep her occupied for days.

'You will eat at twelve o'clock,' said HoofdZuster Grimstra, and sailed away.

The morning went quickly, although by noon Serena realised that she was a little lonely, but the cheerful attempts of the nurses in the dining-room to carry on a conversation with her mitigated that; she went back to her typing and worked with a short break for a cup of milkless tea halfway through the afternoon. Of the doctor there was no sign, but round about four o'clock a porter brought her a bundle of notes to type.

'Written with his left hand and blindfolded,' declared Serena to the empty room. 'I never saw such a scrawl!'

It took her an hour or more to decipher them and render them into neatly typed reports.

She had finished by six o'clock and since there was no sign of the doctor she bore her work down to the lodge. 'Dr ter Feulen,' she said firmly, and handed it over to the porter.

He understood what she was talking about. He took the papers from her, summoned a junior porter, handed them to him and gave him some instructions.

'Dr ter Feulen?' asked Serena, just to be on the safe side.

'Yes, yes, miss. He goes now.' She watched the porter race away, hoping she had done the right thing.

The evening meal was at half-past six; bread and butter, cheese, sausage, cold meat and a salad. She ate it with appetite, carrying on a conversation of sorts with the nurses around her. They were friendly girls; they bore her off presently to a large sitting-room where she watched TV and drank more coffee before going to her bed. It had been quite a nice day, she decided as she jumped into bed, even though she hadn't seen the doctor.

An unseen hand had left more of the manuscript on her desk. She spent the whole of Saturday typing, happy to know that she would be free to do as she liked on Sunday. There was Leeuwarden to explore for a start, and she would find somewhere to have a nice meal. The shops would be shut, of course, but

she could look in the windows... She finished the
last of the typing, tidied her desk, covered her typewriter and gathered her work neatly together. She
would have to take it down to the lodge again, she
supposed; there had been no sign of the doctor.
Probably tied up with his meetings, she decided, and
switched off the lights.

They were switched on again at once. 'Finished?'
asked Dr ter Feulen. 'Splendid. Give me those, if you
please. Be outside the entrance at nine o'clock tomorrow morning.'

'Another hospital?' asked Serena faintly.

'No. We will, I hope, enjoy a few hours' leisure
before we return on Monday.'

'Where?'

'Shall we keep it as a surprise?' he wanted to know
blandly. He stood aside for her to pass him and shut
the door after them both. 'You have been comfortable here?'

'Yes, thank you,' Serena said coldly. 'I was looking
forward to exploring Leeuwarden, I'm not sure that
I——'

'Well, if you're not sure you won't mind post-
poning that until another time, will you?'

They had gone down the staircase together, and now
he turned to go in the opposite direction to her. 'Don't
forget, nine o'clock.' He smiled at her suddenly.
'Goodnight, Serena.'

She marshalled all the reasons she had for not going
with him while she ate some supper and sat with the
nurses watching an old American film. The reasons,
on second thoughts, seemed petty, and moreover she
had earned any treat he might have in store for her.
She would wear the checked skirt and the jacket and

the ivory silk blouse she had most fortunately brought with her. She was still deciding which shoes she should wear when she fell asleep.

It was a fine morning, but cold. Serena dressed, did her face and hair and got into the court shoes. Suede boots would have been the thing, but the court shoes, while probably unsuitable, were unobtrusive.

She had her breakfast, packed her case once more and went downstairs to the forecourt. She had very little idea as to when they were to leave the next morning, so it seemed prudent to leave everything as ready as possible. He had said a few hours, which could mean anything...

The Bentley was drawn up before the entrance and the doctor was deep in conversation with an elderly man. Serena slowed her steps, not sure what to do.

'Good morning, Serena. Come and meet Dr Heringa, he's the director of the hospital.' He turned to the other man. 'My secretary and right arm, Serena Proudfoot.'

She shook hands with the elderly man and said in English, 'Good morning.'

He replied, 'You will enjoy your day, I am sure. I am delighted to meet you, Miss Proudfoot. I will not keep you from your pleasure.' He clapped the doctor on the shoulder. 'I will see you before you go, Marc.'

Serena felt a thrill of pleasure as she settled into her seat. The car was warm and comfortable and she was looking as near her best as it was possible to be. Her euphoria was shortlived.

'You should be wearing a winter coat,' observed her companion carelessly with a sideways glance which bore all the interest of a man looking at a heap of potato sacks.

'Well, I decided not to,' she told him with a snap, 'and what I wear is of no concern to you!'

'My dear girl, don't fly at me like that. And it is my concern; I don't want a secretary with a streaming cold in the head.' He had started the car, but now he stopped and turned to look at her. 'Shall we cry pax?'

Serena said with dignity, 'Certainly, Dr ter Feulen,' and then, forgetting her dignity, 'Where are we going?'

'Ah, wait and see,' was all he would say.

He drove out of Leeuwarden, going north, and presently she saw a signpost to Dokkum. 'Are we going towards the coast?' she ventured.

'Yes.' His rather stern profile gave nothing away, and she decided not to say any more. She knew Dokkum was associated with St Boniface and thus had connections with England. Perhaps he was going to show her something of it. The country was pleasant under a wintry sky and here and there she glimpsed water. There were farms, lying well back from the road, flat-faced and broadly built, connected to the huge barns behind them by a narrow passage. There wasn't much traffic on the road and the villages they went through were quiet.

'Everyone is in church,' said the doctor.

Serena would have liked to have stopped in Dokkum when they reached it; there was a canal running through the centre of the little town, and its old buildings were charming, but the doctor went on, still going north. He had turned off the main road now and was driving along a brick country road, running beside a canal. They drove through two villages, small circles of houses with a church brooding over each of them, and now she could see trees ahead of them, topping a slight rise in the ground.

There was a village tucked into the trees, nicely sheltered from the wide land around it. The church dominated the tiny square and the houses were for the most part small, but every one of them gleamed with paintwork and shining windows, draped in whiter-than-white curtains. In among them were larger houses and what she took to be a miniature town hall opposite the church.

'What a dear little place—like an illustration in a fairy-tale! What is it called?'

'Oosterzum.' They were leaving the village behind and now there were tall iron railings on one side of the road. They curved inwards between stone pillars, and the doctor turned the car between them into a straight drive leading to a large square house, with white walls and green shutters at each of its orderly row of windows.

'Where's this?' asked Serena sharply.

'My home.' He stopped the car before the massive door, undid her seatbelt and then got out to open her door, take her firmly by the arm and go across the gravel just as the house door was thrown open and allowed children, dogs and a number of people to emerge.

'My family,' said the doctor, and gave her a wicked look.

It seemed they were all there. She was introduced to his sisters, four young women, tall, blonde and good-looking with bright blue eyes. 'Talitha, Sanna, Wibekke and Prisca,' said the doctor. 'You can sort them out later.' And he left her for a moment to join his brothers while they shook her hand, all talking at once.

'My brothers; Wilbren, Kaeye and Stendert.'

'Don't bother to remember our names,' the young man called Wilbren said cheerfully, 'and I must warn you that there are more of us inside.'

They bore her indoors with the doctor and his sisters following, but as they entered the hall from the porch he was beside her again.

'Come and meet my mother,' he invited, and crossed the hall—an apartment Serena would dearly have loved to inspect at her leisure, with its lofty ceiling, walls almost covered with paintings in huge ornate frames and a chandelier, dripping cascades of crystal above her head. There was a curving staircase at the back of the hall, but she was given no time to do more than glimpse it.

They went through double doors, solid wood with carved swags of flowers and fruits over their arches, and into a room which was as lofty as the hall and far lighter by reason of the long, wide windows, their velvet curtains echoing the patterned carpet which covered almost the whole floor. Very old, she observed silently, and probably priceless.

There were several people in the room; four men were standing between the windows and there were two young women with them, all tall and good-looking. But the elderly lady coming to meet them wasn't tall, nor was she particularly handsome, moreover, she wasn't much taller than Serena. Her hair was mousy too, as mousy as Serena's own tidy head, but it was streaked with silver and dressed severely in a French pleat. She was dressed with an elegance that didn't detract from her welcoming smile;

she would have looked as nice in a pinny, thought Serena happily.

The doctor bent his great height to kiss his mother. 'Mama, here is Serena. She has been working hard for the last few days and a change of scene seemed a good idea.'

Serena shook the hand held out to her and smiled at the older woman; a nice friendly face, and the blue eyes were gentle.

'My dear, you must think that Marc has brought you to a madhouse! There are so many of us. Whenever he comes to Holland we try to get together here so that we can have a family gathering. Have you brothers and sisters?'

'No, *mevrouw*. I live with my mother.'

'You have a busy life too, I'll be bound.' She turned to the group by the windows. 'Come and meet Serena,' she said, and added, 'Sons-in-law, my dear, and my youngest daughter's fiancé—the two girls are Wilbren and Stendert's wives.' She chuckled. 'There are two adorable babies in the nursery as well as the children running around here.'

It was a lovely day; Serena was passed from one group to the next, talked to, teased a little in the kindest possible way, asked about her work, and after a splendid lunch they took her on a tour of the house and then walked her round the grounds, and all this time she hardly spoke to the doctor. He seemed content to leave her to the friendly care of his brothers and sisters, and after a while she lost her initial shyness and began to enjoy herself enormously. Once or twice she wondered if she were in a dream, for the sight of the doctor, strolling along with one or other of his family, playing with the children, throwing sticks for the dogs, was so alien to her concept of him. There was no sign of his casual coolness, his polite indifference, his confident expectancy that she would do exactly what he wished without argument. He was treating her exactly as he treated his sisters and sister-in-law. Upon reflection Serena was vexed at the thought.

Over tea she had a talk with his mother, a conversation skilfully conducted by that lady which left her in possession of a fair picture of Serena's life. The men went away to play billiards after tea and the women gathered together. The Baronne stitched at her embroidery frame, several of the girls had knitting with them, while the rest sat idle, chatting, careful to include Serena in their talk, and all the while children and dogs and a large black cat wandered from chair to chair. Serena had never been so happy.

The children were borne away to bed presently and the grown-ups had supper: watercress soup, lobster patties, *beignets* and salad and a pavlova to finish. They sat over their coffee, and Serena could have stayed there for hours, just listening to the cheerful hum of talk around her, but the doctor put an end to that.

'Time we went back,' he declared cheerfully. 'We're leaving early in the morning.'

'You'll come again soon?' asked his mother.

'Yes—I'm examining at the Medical School in Groningen in a few weeks' time.'

'And Serena?' Friendly faces beamed at her.

'Me? Oh, I don't suppose I'll come to Holland again...' She caught sight of the doctor's raised eyebrows and hurried on, 'What I mean is, only if the doctor has work for me.'

'Does he drive you hard?' asked Kaeye. 'And do you always call him Doctor?'

'Yes, always.' She smiled because Kaeye was fun, the youngest of the brothers, with an easy friendliness that had melted her shyness.

'Take no notice, Serena,' said the doctor from the head of the table. He sounded amused. 'And do call me Marc if you would like to.'

She said thoughtfully, 'Thank you, but I don't think it would do. I might forget in hospital and that wouldn't be very nice for you.'

'I quite agree,' chimed in the Baronne. 'Marc wouldn't have a patient left if everyone addressed him so. Doctors have a certain mystique...' There was a howl of laughter from everyone at the table. When it had died down, she went on calmly, 'Not for me, of course, but there are still any number of people who think of the medical profession as a race apart.'

There was more laughter as the doctor got to his feet. 'You're undermining my ego,' he observed. 'It is a good thing I'm not operating tomorrow, I've lost all my self-assurance!'

There was more laughter as they all trooped into the hall, while Serena got into her jacket and went round shaking hands with everyone.

'I've had such a lovely day,' she said to the Baronne. 'I'm going to remember it forever... I had no idea...'

Her hostess kissed her cheek. 'I'm very glad you came, my dear, and I hope that one day perhaps you will come and see us all again.'

Serena, getting into the Bentley, reflected that there was nothing she would like more, but she supposed it was politeness on the part of her hostess, kindly meant, in the same way as her mother so often begged a chance-met friend to come to tea one day without meaning it at all.

The doctor had nothing much to say, merely wanted to know if she was tired, reminding her that he intended to leave at eight o'clock the following morning, and beyond a few remarks about the darkness of the evening and their prospects for a speedy journey back to England he had nothing to add. He was his usual self once more, retreated into his bland and distant shell. She sighed gently; the glimpse she had had of him had been exciting.

Everyone had seen them off. They lingered on the steps outside the porch, watching the tail-lights disappear round the bend in the road.

The Baronne turned to go into the house. 'A very sweet girl,' she observed. 'She will do very well.'

'Mama, you matchmaker!' said Talitha. 'She is just right, though.'

'Of course she is, my dear.'

'But Marc isn't . . .'

'Marc wishes her to be happy, he is concerned for her but he does not want to show it. He has been in love many times, I am sure, but to love as well as being in love, that is something else. He is not yet aware . . .'

'And Serena?'

'Ah, she does not expect to be loved and so she is also unaware.' The Baronne took Talitha's arm. 'We shall see.'

They went indoors and the elderly Hans, who had served the family for almost all his life, shut the door behind them. 'A nice young lady the baron brought home,' he said in Fries with the respectful familiarity of an old and trusted servant. 'Tiele thinks the same, *mevrouw.*'

The Baronne paused by him. 'You are both right, Hans—a charming young lady.' She put a hand on his sleeve. 'Let us hope that we see more of her.'

At the hospital the doctor got out of the car and went with Serena into the entrance hall. She stopped inside the door to look up at him.

'Thank you for my lovely day, Doctor. I can't remember when I've enjoyed myself so much, and your family were so kind.' She added shyly, 'I don't know much about large families—they must be tremendous fun.'

He had taken her hand in his. 'They are. I'm glad that you were happy with us.'

'I'll never forget it. Goodnight, Doctor.' She turned away and paused. 'Ought I to call you Baron? I didn't know you were so—so important! One of your sisters—no, it was a sister-in-law, I think—said that you were the head of the family and that the house and grounds and several farms were yours and your people had lived there for hundreds of years.'

'That would be Sebbie, the chatterbox. And don't ever dare to call me Baron, Serena. That's all very well in Friesland but unthinkable in hospital.'

His words were severe, but uttered in such a kindly voice that she smiled widely at him.

It was raining when they left the next morning, with a chilly wind blowing in from the Waddenzee, but the car was warm and Serena settled into her comfortable seat, prepared for a long drive. The doctor had told her that he intended driving to Boulogne. Once they were on their way he told her more. 'We shall go over the Afsluitdijk and down to Amsterdam, then Utrecht, south to Antwerp and across to Boulogne.'

'It will take all day?'

'Not in this car. I hope you will be home by late afternoon, possibly before that. We shall stop for coffee north of Amsterdam and have lunch round about Breda, but if you want to stop you mustn't hesitate to say so.'

They drove in silence for a time, rushing across the *dijk*, swallowing the miles to the other side. 'Take the day off tomorrow,' said the doctor presently. 'I won't be going into the hospital and you will be glad of some time to yourself.'

'Thank you.' She sought for something else to say and could think of nothing sensible. She sat looking out at the wet countryside, conscious that she was reluctant to leave Holland. Partly, she had to admit, because she had had a glimpse of what life could be like if one lived in a lovely old house surrounded by a family who seemed to enjoy their lives.

They stopped in Hoorn for their coffee. The Keizerskroon Hotel was old and its restaurant was pleasant and warm, but Serena wasn't allowed to linger, and within twenty minutes they were on their way again.

There was a good deal of traffic on the road by now, all moving fast, and the nearer they got to Amsterdam the busier it began to be. They didn't go into the city but took the ring road that joined the motorway to Utrecht. They avoided that city and drove on to Breda. South of the town the doctor stopped in Princehage. 'There's a restaurant here— the Mirabelle. You must be hungry.' He turned to smile at her. 'I know I am!'

They lunched with good appetites; *erwtensoep*, grilled sole, and finished their meal with *poffertjes* and a pot of coffee and, much refreshed, got back into the car once again.

'Not long now,' observed the doctor. 'You're not tired?'

Even if she had been she wouldn't have said so. He had planned the trip to get them back by a certain time, and to delay him wouldn't do at all. They swept on to Antwerp, Lille and finally Boulogne.

It was still raining and the afternoon was dwindling into a miserable dusk. The doctor had timed his journey accurately. They went aboard the Hoverspeed within half an hour, and Serena heaved a sigh of relief at the sight of the tea she was offered. It seemed to her that they were at Dover in no time at all. They went through Customs without hindrance and slid with deceptive speed up the motorway on the last leg of their journey.

They had spoken very little, but the silence had been a comfortable one. As they slowed through the suburbs Serena said, 'Are you going to the hospital? Would you mind putting me down there, please?'

'I'm not going there. I'll drop you off at your home.' He spoke in a voice she had learned not to argue with, and anyway, it would be nice to be taken right to her door.

East Sheen contrasted badly with Oosterzum, and the house looked small and uninviting as the doctor stopped before its door. There were no lights showing and he asked sharply, 'Is there no one at home? Does your mother not know that you are coming back today?'

'Well, I tried to get her on the phone yesterday and the day before that, but I dare say she was out ... I

expect she's visiting friends; she'll be back for supper.'
She undid her seatbelt, and he got out of the car,
opened her door and got her case from the boot.

'I don't like to leave you alone——' he began, but
she interrupted him briskly.

'I often come home when Mother is out, please
don't worry.'

All the same, he took the door key from her and
opened the door and followed her into the house,
turning on lights as he went. The rooms were tidy,
but there was no sign of a welcome, no tray laid, no
sign of a meal prepared. He said slowly, 'I think you
had better come with me and I'll bring you back later
when your mother is home.'

She said vigorously, 'That's kind of you, but quite
unnecessary—I'm fine.'

'You want me to go?'

'Yes, I do.' As she uttered the words she knew them
for a lie. She didn't want him to go; suddenly the
thought of not seeing him for even one day was
unbearable. Of course she didn't want him to go, she
wanted him to stay with her for the rest of her life.
It was a shock to discover that she loved him, and she
said feverishly, 'Do please go—and thank you for
bringing me home.'

'If that is what you want.' He stood close to her,
staring down into her face. 'I shall telephone later to
make sure that you're all right.' He swooped suddenly and kissed her hard, then went out of the door
into his car and drove away.

She closed the door and stood in the hall, getting
over the shock of the kiss. Why had he kissed her?
she wondered, and then caught a glimpse of her face
in the hall looking-glass. It gave her the answer; she
looked pale and tired and her hair was untidy, her

nose shone—she was an object of pity. The kiss, she felt sure, had been given in the same spirit as a kindly man would have stroked a forlorn kitten or patted a lost puppy. Two tears dripped down her cheeks and she wiped them away with a gloved hand, leaving a grubby smear on her cheeks.

Crying wasn't going to help: she went to her room and unpacked her case, tidied herself and went to the kitchen to put the kettle on. Tea and toast would make her feel better. The house was cold and she stayed in the kitchen to drink her tea. Obviously her mother hadn't expected her; perhaps her letter had never arrived. She got up and went into the sitting-room, turned on the gas fire and looked around her. Her letter was on one of the lamp tables. She picked it up and reread it; there were just a few lines to remind her mother of the day on which she would return. She went upstairs then and looked in her mother's bedroom, which was much as usual, and she went downstairs again to drink her tea.

When she heard the front door open she got up and went into the hall. Her mother was taking off her coat.

'Darling, there you are!' She shivered. 'This house is icy—I shall catch a chill.'

Serena kissed her. 'Did you forget I was coming home, Mother?'

'Well, no, not really, darling, but I'd made arrangements I didn't want to break.' She laughed suddenly. 'I've got a surprise for you, Serena. I'm going to marry Mr Harding—Arthur!'

CHAPTER SIX

SERENA was silent for so long that Mrs Proudfoot said petulantly, 'Well, aren't you going to wish me happy?'

'Yes, of course, Mother. I hope you'll be very happy. Do tell me all about it.' She smiled, and it felt as though her face had cracked. 'Come into the sitting-room—I lit the fire.'

Her mother sat down in an easy chair. 'You're surprised, I suppose. But you were so wrapped up in your work,' she sounded accusing, 'there seemed no point in talking to you about it. Anyway, it has all turned out so well. Arthur—Mr Harding—has a house in Shropshire, near Ludlow, and you'll be able to spend your holidays there. He's staying in London for a few more days. We shall be married by special licence—there's no point in waiting. I've put this house up for sale...'

She saw Serena's look of simply dismayed astonishment. 'You can have some of the money to rent a small flat. You'll like that, darling—to lead your own life and have fun with your friends.' She leaned forward, brimful of her news. 'There's already someone waiting to buy this place. He'll let me know tomorrow. You can have what furniture you want, of course.' She gave her tinkling laugh. 'Darling, you'll have to go flat-hunting—can you get some days off?'

'Only tomorrow——' Serena broke off as the phone rang. She had forgotten that the doctor had said he would phone. She got up to answer it, and when she did he said,

'Serena? Is your mother back?'

She answered steadily, 'Yes, Doctor. Thank you for ringing.'

'What's the matter?'

'Nothing.' She had thought her voice sounded as it always did. 'I dare say I'm tired.'

'Then go to bed. I shall want you in Outpatients at eight o'clock the day after tomorrow.'

'Very well, Doctor. Goodnight.'

His 'goodnight' was terse before he hung up.

Her mother asked without much interest, 'Who was that? The doctor? Did you tell him about me?'

'No, Mother. Where will you be married?'

'Oh, at the local register office. I've bought the sweetest outfit—pearl-grey wool with such a pretty blouse. You'll come, of course...'

'When is it to be?'

'Next week—Thursday. We shall drive straight to Ludlow. Isn't it exciting, darling?' Mrs Proudfoot became faintly accusing. 'Of course you don't understand what I've suffered, living here all alone doing the shopping and the housework and the cooking...'

'But, Mother, I've been living here too...' She almost added, And I've done most of the shopping and cleaning and cooking.

'Oh, I know that, but you've had an interesting job and met young men and women of your own age.' Mrs Proudfoot was getting rapidly crosser. 'Though much good it's done you—you've never once brought anyone back here. Oh, I know Dr ter Feulen came, but you're hardly his type. I dare say he's able to take his pick of pretty girls.'

Serena agreed silently to this, but all she said, in a soothing voice, was, 'Are there going to be many guests at the wedding?'

'Oh, friends—Arthur has no immediate family, thank goodness, and nor have we, only your father's elder sister, who hates me anyway.'

'Aunt Edith? She's actually married to the rector of a village in Dorset, isn't she?'

'Great Canning. I haven't heard from them since your father died.'

Serena decided it wasn't the right moment to tell her mother that Aunt Edith wrote to her from time to time. Stiff letters without much news, but at least she had kept in touch, and Serena had answered them.

Her mother yawned. 'I shall go to bed. I'm quite exhausted, but Arthur insisted on taking me out to dinner.' She dropped a kiss on Serena's cheek. 'Bring me some warm milk when I've had my bath, darling. I must keep my strength up for another busy day tomorrow,' she added in a satisfied voice. 'I'm almost certain that man is going to buy the house.'

Serena went to the kitchen and fetched the milk for her mother from the fridge and poured it into a saucepan. It was a good thing she had something to do, for she seemed unable to think sensibly. She remembered that her mother hadn't asked her about her journey or shown any interest in her trip to Leeuwarden. She smiled a little then. It must seem very unimportant to her mother with such an upheaval taking place. She carried the milk upstairs, locked the door and closed the windows, then went to her own bed. She hadn't realised she was cold. She lay in a hot bath, making herself review the situation sensibly. Tomorrow would be a busy day. There would be her clothes to press, blouses to wash and iron, her hair to wash too. She mustn't lose sight of her job, it merited a neat appearance at all times and she couldn't risk slacking in any way. Her mother had talked about a flat, but she would never be able to afford the rent of even a modest place. It would have to be a furnished flatlet or something similar. Perhaps she would be able to take some of the smaller furniture with her and store the rest if her mother didn't want it.

She got into bed and lay thinking. It was no good worrying about the more distant future, the thing was to find somewhere quickly and hang on to her job. Her mother hadn't suggested that she should find work near Ludlow, and even if she had Serena would have refused, for that would mean that she would never see Marc again. She smiled to herself in the dark, remembering her day at his home; just for a moment her thoughts were happy, and she closed her eyes and went to sleep in the middle of them.

She was up early and breakfasted alone, for as her mother sleepily pointed out when she took her a cup of tea, 'As you're home, darling, you might spoil me a little. I should love my breakfast in bed.'

Serena had tidied the house, washed her smalls and was pressing her skirt when the prospective buyer arrived. He was pleasant and very polite and businesslike, and he had made up his mind. He went over the house again, pronounced it just what he and his wife were looking for and said that he would go at once to his solicitor. Mrs Proudfoot, over the coffee Serena had made, pressed him for a date. 'I'm remarrying,' she told him prettily, 'and I should be so glad to have the matter settled before we leave here.'

The man glanced at Serena. 'Your daughter is going with you?'

'No, oh, no—she has a marvellous job at one of the hospitals here, we shall find her a nice little flat.' She spoke with such conviction that Serena believed her. There would be enough money to buy something modest; the house was being sold for a substantial sum.

When the man had gone she asked, 'Had I better start flat-hunting, Mother? Shall we go together?'

'I'm going out to lunch with Arthur—he'll be here in half an hour. You go by all means, darling, see if you can find somewhere that you can afford out of your salary.'

'To buy? Mother, you know I've almost no money of my own, I couldn't afford a mortgage.' She went on quietly, 'I heard you telling that man you were going to buy me a flat...'

'Did I? I was too excited to know what I was saying. I've talked it over with Arthur; he thought we ought to get somewhere for you, but I pointed out how independent you were. You'd much rather have a rented place of your own, wouldn't you, darling? Then if you want to move or get another job, you could do so easily. You can have any of the small furniture— the big stuff will all go with the house. You've ample time to find something—it'll be a while before they can take over. Of course you can stay here until then unless you find something in the meantime.' She sighed. 'Darling, do stop fussing about yourself! I have so much to think of, and that's Arthur at the door now and I'm not ready.'

She hurried up to her room, and Serena opened the door and invited Mr Harding in. He was a nice man, easygoing to a fault, but kind. He asked about her work, and since from what he said she gathered that he imagined that her future had been nicely settled, she forbore from mentioning it. Once she was alone in the house she sat down with pencil and paper. Writing everything down might help her to make sensible plans—as it was, the half-baked ideas running round and round in her head were useless, for all she was really thinking about was Marc. She wouldn't tell him, that was something she was quite sure of. She wrote it down and underlined the note before making a list of the likely streets near the hospital. Without help she would have to settle for a flatlet or even a bed-sitter. Her salary was quite good now and she had a little money in the bank, but there was the future to think of. Marc might go back to Holland and it might be difficult to get another job. The very idea sent her heart plummeting.

Over a pot of tea she decided what to do and not waste time about it. It was nearly lunchtime and the buses were almost empty; she caught one that stopped close to the hospital and began to search for somewhere to live.

She ignored the shabbier streets close to the hospital and turned her attention to the small side streets, most of them culs-de-sac, lined with tall houses with basements and from the number of bells beside their doors occupied by several occupants. Quite forgetful of lunch, she walked up and down each street. Any one of them would do—within ten minutes' walk of the hospital, as quiet a neighbourhood as one could expect in that part of London and a shopping street close by. Only there was nothing vacant. She made her way to the shops and studied the cards in a newsagent's window. It was a nice surprise to find several vacancies in the streets she had explored. She studied them carefully and chose one that might do. For one thing, it mentioned the fact that it was close to the hospital, which might mean that the other occupants were nurses or staff from the Royal, and the description, even taken with a pinch of salt, sounded possible. A large room at the back of the house with use of the garden, partly furnished with kitchenette and shower. The rent would take a good deal of her salary, but it might be worth that; it was going to be her home, after all.

She had a cup of coffee and a sandwich in a small café next to the newsagent's, then walked briskly to the rather inaptly named Primrose Bank in Park Street. There wasn't a park within miles either.

There were several bells, and since she had no idea which one to ring she thumped the knocker. The door was opened with something of a flourish by a tall thin woman who could have been any age between forty and sixty. She had a forbidding cast of feature, but she was nicely dressed in a nondescript fashion and her voice, although brisk, was quiet.

'Yes? You want to see me? I own the house—Mrs Peck.' She stood aside.

'You have a flatlet, Mrs Peck?' began Serena. 'Is it still to let?'

For answer she was waved into the hall, which was long and narrow and rather dark. 'This way.' Mrs Peck walked rapidly to the back of the hall and opened a door. There were a few steps beyond it and another door. 'Semi-basement,' she said over her shoulder as she opened it.

It was a good deal better than Serena had hoped for, with two windows overlooking a rather neglected strip of garden and a stout door beside them. The room was rather dark, but the walls were distempered and it was very clean. The kitchenette, poky and dark, was spotless too, with a small sink and an even smaller cooking stove. The shower was an elongated cupboard but adequate. Serena walked slowly round, looking at the furniture; bare necessities, a divan against one wall, a small table, two chairs and some bookshelves. Mrs Peck said with a touch of belligerence, 'The advert says partly furnished.'

'I've some small bits of furniture—you wouldn't mind if I had it here? I work at the Royal, they'll give you a reference...'

'Don't need one. I've got three nurses in the first-floor flat. It's weekly paid in advance and you pay your own gas. The electric lights come in the rent.'

'Can I use the garden? There is a way to the street from here?'

'Yes, but it's kept locked—can't have prowlers. You're on your own?'

'Yes. Would you object to a cat if I got one later on?'

'Not that I know of, as long as it keeps to itself.'

'Then I'd like to come, Mrs Peck. I'm not sure when I'm moving. May I pay you a week's rent now and arrange for all my things to be delivered some time within a week?'

'Suits me.'

Serena went back home and found the house empty. She was hungry and a bit excited, and once she had made herself a meal of sorts she took pencil and paper once more and went round the house, choosing what she hoped her mother would let her take with her. That done, she went and sat down, no longer thinking of the day's happenings but of Marc. He would be home, she supposed, and she wondered where home was. A flat in one of those expensive blocks on the other side of London? A house? He wouldn't need a house just for himself, but could he bear to live in a flat, however large, after the spacious comfort of his home in Friesland?

'What a waste of time,' she told the empty room, 'worrying about him; he's more than capable of looking after himself and getting what he wants, and it's me I should be worrying about.' Which, though erring in grammar, was right.

It was late evening when her mother returned. Serena heard the car stop outside the house, but Mr Harding didn't come in this time. Her mother had had a splendid day; she went over every detail of it, and only when she had exhausted every aspect of it did she ask perfunctorily, 'And you, darling? Have you had fun?'

'I've rented a flatlet near the Royal—in Park Street. Quite nice, and it opens on to the back garden. It's partly furnished . . .'

'Oh, good. You must choose a few bits and pieces from here, Serena. When do you plan to move?'

'As soon as the things I choose can be collected and delivered. Will you miss me, Mother?' She hadn't meant to dwell on that.

'Miss you? Well, of course I shall, darling, but you must come and see us when you have a holiday, and of course we shall come up to town from time to time. You must be very excited at the idea of having a place of your own.'

Serena told herself that her mother didn't mean to be unkind or thoughtless—perhaps she really did think that living in a poky room on one's own was fun. 'I made a list,' she said, 'if you would take a look?'

She watched her mother scan the list. 'Darling, you do want a lot, don't you? Still, I suppose you can have them, they're not worth much. Don't take the good china, though, will you? It's quite valuable, and there's that little man in the antique shop in Richmond who'll give me a good price for it.'

Serena said, 'Very well, Mother,' in a colourless voice. All these years, she reflected with surprise, I've done my best to look after her and love her, and it hasn't meant a thing to her. I'd feel better about it if I were younger and pretty. She gave herself a mental shake. She was a sensible girl and she despised self-pity. Probably life would be quite exciting once she had settled into Primrose Bank. She said out loud, 'I shall get a cat——'

Her mother laughed. 'Oh, Serena, old maids have cats!'

Serena said cheerfully. 'But I am an old maid, Mother. Now could you tell me about the wedding? I'll get time off to come.'

'Two o'clock at the Richmond Register Office and, afterwards, Richmond Hill Hotel, just for a drink and to cut the cake before we leave.'

Surely the doctor wouldn't object to her having a few hours off in the afternoon? She could stay late if there was a lot to do... It was quite a journey from the Royal. She would have to take the Underground, her lunch hour was one o'clock, so all she needed were three hours tacked on to that. She remembered suddenly that she hadn't given her mother a wedding present, and she would have to arrange for the things she had chosen to be collected.

There was no time for that the next morning. She got to the hospital with only minutes to spare and was sitting at her desk, a bit breathless, when Mrs Dunn poked her head round the door of the little room Serena had been given to work in. 'Back, are you?' she asked needlessly. 'Did he work you hard? Miss Payne was always exhausted.'

'I worked hard, but I'm not tired, Mrs Dunn.'

'Well, that's a good thing—he's got a backlog of work from here to there. He's got an extra Outpatients' this morning, you're to be there by half-past eight.' Her eye sought the clock on the wall. 'It's twenty past eight now.'

'So it is,' agreed Serena gravely. Mrs Dunn had an aptitude for stating the obvious. 'I'll be there. Mrs Dunn, I'd like the afternoon of Thursday week off— will that be all right with you if I get Dr ter Feulen's permission?'

'Suits me—you don't work for anyone else but him. He won't be best pleased—he likes everyone to be at his beck and call.'

That, thought Serena, was only too true. She would have to go to the wedding whatever he said. He would, however, she hoped, be in a good temper.

Good temper, for the moment at any rate, had eluded the doctor. He greeted her cheerful good morning with a rumbling grunt which might have been anything in any language. Later, at the end of a long morning, he strode away, uttering no more than his punctilious thanks to those who had been working with him.

Something would have to be done about that, thought Serena, skipping down to the canteen to devour mince, potatoes and unspecified greens. 'And you're lucky to get that,' declared the cross-faced woman who served her, 'coming late like this—you ought to know better.'

'Try telling that to Dr ter Feulen,' said Serena, her mouth full.

She typed without pause until five o'clock, and, when the porter's lodge phoned to tell her that she was to hand in her work to Sister's office on Men's Surgical since Dr ter Feulen would be there, she sat down and composed a note requesting a free afternoon on Thursday week for urgent family reasons. She clipped it to the top of her typing and took it downstairs, and just to be on the safe side in case he should be there and think of something else he wanted done, she put on her outdoor things.

He was there, squashed in with Sister, his registrar and a pile of notes, busy writing what Serena had no doubt were sapient instructions which no one would be able to decipher without the aid of a magnifying glass and a medical dictionary.

She laid the papers down on the desk, wished everyone good evening and whisked herself away. By the morning he would have had time to read it and have got used to the idea.

She had reached the entrance when he fetched up beside her, breathing normally, although he must have gone like the wind. She had overlooked the fact that he was a very large man with long legs; he probably knew some short cuts too. She pretended that he wasn't there and put out a hand to push the door open. He took the hand in his and gave it back to her.

'What's all this?' His voice was so mild that she prepared herself for an argument.

'Is it not clear?' she asked politely. 'I would like an afternoon off on Thurs——'

'I can read that. Why?'

'Urgent family business.'

She glanced at him and saw that he expected a reason. Family business, after all, could be anything from a grandmother's funeral to failure to pay the rates. She said gently, 'I hardly think it would interest you, Doctor; a family wedding.'

Just for a moment the look on his face baffled her, but it had gone again, smoothed into his usual blandness. 'Yours?'

'Certainly not!'

'Take the afternoon off by all means.' He held the door open for her. 'There will probably be a backlog of work when you get back.'

'Well, yes, I know.' She gave him a wide smile. 'Thank you very much, Doctor. Goodnight.'

The door was open, but she couldn't get past him unless she trod on his feet. He stood looking down at her and then smiled suddenly so that her heart turned over and took her breath. He watched the slow colour creep into her cheeks before he stood aside and she scuttled past him.

Her mother was home, sitting at her desk, writing. 'There you are, darling, just in time to make me a cup of tea. I've been so busy all day.'

That makes two of us, thought Serena naughtily, but she took off her things and went to the kitchen, where she got a tea-tray ready and presently took it back to the sitting-room.

'Arthur's been so kind,' said her mother. 'I know you'll be grateful; he's arranged for the things you want for your flat to be collected and delivered; they're coming in the morning. I expect you're dying to get settled in.'

Serena agreed pleasantly. 'I'll pack my things on Saturday and Sunday and go there on Monday after work.' She added with unconscious wistfulness, 'Unless you'd like me to stay until the wedding?'

Mrs Proudfoot spoke hastily. 'Of course not, darling, I'd be the last one to hinder you. In fact, I thought you might have wanted to move before the weekend...'

'I'm working.'

'Of course—how silly I am!' She gave a little laugh. 'There's so much to do, it's so fortunate that Arthur's here to help me—you know how helpless I am about business.' She sipped her tea and nibbled a biscuit. 'Don't forget, darling, that you'll always be welcome at Ludlow.' She put down her cup. 'I almost forgot—we're going away for Christmas and the New Year. Arthur thinks a warm climate will do me good. You know I can never stand the miserable winters we have here, but I dare say you'll have a lovely time. Are there other young people in the other flats?'

Serena just stopped herself in time from reminding her mother that a flatlet wasn't a flat, it was a bed-sitter, gone upmarket. 'Some nurses from the Royal.'

'There, didn't I say so?' Mrs Proudfoot sounded triumphant. 'I knew you'd find something to please you. A pity that I simply haven't the time to come and see it before we go... Still, I did tell you we'll come to town from time to time, and you won't want visitors until you've settled in.'

Serena poured second cups and her mother said presently, 'I did mention that I'd let you have some money for a flat, Serena. You have enough to go on with, haven't you? It will be some time before the money is dealt with, but I won't forget; if you're in dire straits you might let me know.'

The week wound its busy way to a close, and beyond brief instructions as to her work, good mornings and good evenings and his usual courteous thanks at the end of them, Dr ter Feulen had nothing to say to Serena, and, being a sensible girl, she had hardly expected anything else.

She spent her weekend packing her possessions and on the Saturday went to Park Street to arrange the furniture which had been delivered. The room looked much better once she had disposed the small easy chair, the lamp table and the colourful rug from the dining-room which her mother had never liked. She spent the afternoon hanging one or two pictures, arranging her china and kitchen equipment, putting up lampshades and making up the divan and covering it with a bedspread from her room at East Sheen, then, still with time to spare, she went to the shops and stocked up on basic food, arranged for the milkman to deliver and bought a bunch of dahlias in vivid reds and golds. It would do very well, she told herself, and she had been lucky to find it, and at a fairly reasonable rent too. She closed the door, put the key in her pocket and took a bus back to East Sheen.

Her mother had said she would be home on Sunday. Mr Harding had to drive down to Tunbridge Wells to see an old friend and she had declared prettily that she wanted to spend the day with Serena. But she wasn't there when Serena got back; instead there was a note on the kitchen table. Arthur had called and persuaded her that a quiet weekend in the country was just what she needed. 'So we shall be back tomorrow in the early evening,' the note ended, 'and we can all have supper together.'

So Serena was faced with a Saturday evening with nothing to do but watch TV, wash her hair and go to bed with a book, and since she was on her own there wasn't much point in getting up early on Sunday morning. She pottered around the house, read the Sunday papers, did her nails and made a cake. There was still a lot of the day left. Her mother had said they would have supper, all of them together, so perhaps she should do something about that. She poked around the fridge and larder and assembled the ingredients for a quiche and a salad, and then went to her room to make sure that she had packed everything in the case she had left for the last-minute items. She would have to take it with her on the bus in the morning.

The evening was well advanced when her mother and Mr Harding returned.

'Darling,' called her mother, 'we're here at last! It was so late that we stopped and had dinner on the way back—I knew you wouldn't mind. Did you cook yourself something?'

Serena came out of the kitchen, kissed her mother and wished Mr Harding good evening. 'No,' she said equably, 'I understood you'd both be back and we'd be having supper together, but don't worry, I can boil an egg.'

She met Mr Harding's faintly worried look with a pleasant smile and went back to the kitchen, where she gave vent to her outraged feelings by hurling eggs, milk and butter into a saucepan and scrambling eggs. Then she cleared the table she had set so carefully and fetched a tray, made a salad and dished up the eggs. There was sherry in the kitchen dresser. She fetched the bottle and a glass and tossed off a glass, then refilled it. She was halfway through the eggs when Mrs Proudfoot came into the kitchen.

'Darling, I thought you were making coffee...'

Serena took a good sip of sherry. 'I'm having my supper, Mother.' She said it cheerfully, but she wished above all things to burst into tears and wallow in self-pity. Instead she daringly poured a third glass of sherry; she would be sorry for that later, but it did give her Dutch courage. And that reminded her of Dr ter Feulen; she would see him in the morning, and that was something to look forward to. She finished her eggs while her mother made the coffee, muttering in a hurt way about the ingratitude of children and how exhausted she was. Serena, deep in thoughts of Marc, scarcely heard her.

She took her mother a cup of tea before she left in the morning, with the assurance that she would be at the register office on Thursday.

Rather belatedly Mrs Proudfoot wanted to know how she was to manage until then. 'I shall have to cope alone,' she uttered helplessly. 'I suppose you couldn't pop in after work? I've got all my packing to do...'

Serena said firmly that no, she couldn't, at the same time reflecting that she was becoming very hard-hearted. 'I don't leave until half-past five or six o'clock, Mother, and by the time I got here it would be time for me to go back to Park Street.'

She kissed her parent, reiterated her promise to be at the wedding and took herself off to work burdened with her case.

Dr ter Feulen was distantly polite in his manner when she went to his clinic. She could only assume that he had thought better of inviting her to his home and was anxious to let her see that. It shattered her loving heart, but pride stiffened her. Let him be as distant and polite as he wished. Two could play at that game!

Not that there was any time to play at anything. Her small beaky nose was kept to the grindestone all day. She handed in the last of her work just before six o'clock, but this time she left it in the empty consultant's room, and with the case dragging heavily, made for home. He was standing just outside the entrance, impervious to the cold evening, talking to his registrar, and as she slipped past he turned to speak to her.

'Going home, Serena? My regards to your mother.'

She thanked him and hurried away before he could say anything else, then remembered just in time that her usual bus-stop for East Sheen was on the right of the hospital entrance. Now she would travel in the opposite direction, and if he happened to be looking he might wonder...

She turned right towards the East Sheen bus as if to join its queue, and then slid her way behind it, crossed the street and caught a bus which would take her the short distance to Park Street. She would walk in future, she decided, sitting squashed between two ladies exchanging details of their operations just as though she were not there. The exercise would be good for her and she would save the fare.

Primrose Bank didn't look too bad as she climbed the two steps to its front door and unlocked it; there were lights on in most of the windows and it was pleasant and warm as she went in. Her own room didn't look too bad either. She went and switched on the lights, turned on the gas fire and drew the curtains, took off her coat and got herself some supper. She looked around her as she ate; the chairs and tables she had brought with her fitted in very nicely and the TV set, which at the last moment her mother had rather grudgingly agreed to her having, gave the room a pleasant appearance of being lived in. She washed up, put everything ready for the morning and switched on the nine o'clock news. Only later, when she was in bed, she had the frightening feeling that she had been uprooted. There was nothing left of her former life; she would have to start again.

'And I will too!' she declared loudly and defiantly.

It was on the Wednesday, just as she was packing up for the day, that Dr ter Feulen walked into her room. His abrupt, 'What is the matter, Serena?' took her quite by surprise, so that she just sat silent, goggling at him.

'Matter?' she managed after a silence which just had to be broken. 'What should be the matter? Nothing.'

He shrugged his shoulders. 'Never mind, I shall find out.'

She said strongly, 'There's nothing to find . . .'

He smiled. It wasn't a nice smile, she considered. She remembered that he had told her never to lie to him and although it wasn't much of a fib she felt guilty.

He watched her blush. 'I believe I told you never to fib to me, Serena, so I shouldn't waste time doing it if I were you.'

She was startled that he had read her thoughts, but she couldn't think of anything to say to that. He went away without another word and left her sitting there with the nagging thought that he might be able to discover about her mother remarrying, but on consideration she didn't see how he could find out. She went back to her room and laid her clothes ready for the wedding on the morrow.

Her winter coat was by no means new, but the jacket would look all wrong with the green jersey dress; there was a velvet beret to go with the coat and her shoes and gloves were good. She busied herself polishing the furniture and tried not to think about the doctor.

It was a cold bright day the next morning. She worked feverishly all the morning to get as much done as possible, and for once stopped typing at noon precisely. She had eaten a sandwich with the morning coffee and there was no need to stop for lunch. She caught a bus and got to the register office in good time.

Her mother looked charming and very pretty. Mr Harding had given her a pale mink coat and she carried a bunch of violets. There were a dozen or so guests at the ceremony. Serena knew them all, and at the hotel, over the canapés and wine, she laughed and chatted and agreed that her mother looked as young as her daughter and what a lucky girl she was to have such a splendid job—and a flat. They nodded and smiled at her and said that they had heard all about it from her mother.

Mr Harding bore his bride away after an hour or two and everyone went home. It was almost four o'clock by now and Serena had to wait for a bus, and when she did get one it stopped every few yards, so that she was in a fine state of fidgets by the time she got to the Royal. Most of the clerical staff had already gone home, but she had said that she would finish any work there was. She uncovered her typewriter, took off her coat and beret, flung them over a chair and sat down.

The doctor had taken her at her word. There was a good-sized pile of notes to be typed up. Serena set to work.

CHAPTER SEVEN

MARC TER FEULEN had splendid eyesight. He had seen Serena dodging behind the bus queue, weighed down by the case she was lugging with her. She was up to something, and he found himself wondering what it was and, moreover, anxious to find out, but it wasn't until the day after the wedding that he found the time to satisfy his curiosity.

It was almost seven o'clock when he got into the Bentley and drove himself to East Sheen. Serena would be home by now, although at the back of his mind was the vague doubt that she wasn't.

There were lights streaming from all the windows as he stopped the car, got out of it and rang the doorbell. The young woman who came to the door certainly wasn't Serena. She looked at him enquiringly and he asked with inborn authority, nicely mingled with courtesy, 'Mrs Proudfoot no longer lives here?'

'Got married yesterday and gone to live somewhere—Ludlow, I believe.' She eyed him with faint suspicion. 'Are you a friend of hers?'

He put out a large hand. 'Dr ter Feulen. I've been out of the country for a few weeks. I had no idea that she was marrying again. Serena—her daughter?'

He saw the faint suspicion leave her face. 'Oh, you're a doctor. Well, I suppose it's all right to tell you where Miss Proudfoot has gone. Went ever so quickly too, but Mrs Proudfoot sold this house without telling her, so my husband said, so she had to find something.' She held the door open. 'Come into the hall, I'll find the address for you.'

When she came back with it she said doubtfully, 'I suppose it's all right letting you have it? It's near the Royal Hospital.'

The doctor said gently, 'If you would prefer that I shouldn't have it I can get it easily from the Royal. I—er—know several people on the staff.'

'Well, of course you would, being a doctor.' She handed him the paper. 'A nice young lady, my husband said, and very quiet.'

He agreed gravely. 'She will doubtless tell me all about the wedding.' He smiled at her, shook hands and wished her a goodnight and got back into the Bentley.

He was hungry and tired, for he had had a busy day and there was no reason why he should spend what should have been a quiet evening tracking down Serena. 'Tiresome girl,' he muttered as he drove back the way he had come.

There was a fine drizzle falling and Park Street, dimly lighted, its pavements glistening with wet, looked depressing. The houses looked depressing too, even though they were for the most part well kept. He stopped outside Primrose Bank and examined the row of cards by the bells. The bottom one was blank, so he thumped the knocker.

Mrs Peck opened the door on its chain. Her 'Yes?' was brisk and unfriendly.

'I am so sorry to have disturbed you,' said the doctor, at his most urbane. 'I've come to call on Miss Proudfoot. Dr ter Feulen from the Royal Hospital.'

Mrs Peck took the door off its chain and bade him come in. It was interesting, he felt, how the mention of the word doctor put people at their ease. 'She's got the basement room.' She led the way to the door at the back of the hall and opened it, nodding at the further door. 'That's it.'

He thanked her, and she shut the door behind him as he knocked on the further door. Serena had opened a tin of beans for her supper and just put the saucepan on the little stove. She turned off the gas and with the saucepan in her hand went to open the door. Mrs Peck had said earlier that evening that she would leave another saucepan for her and that would be it, she supposed.

The doctor was leaning against a wall, and all she could think of to say was, 'I was expecting Mrs Peck with a saucepan.'

He swept her quite gently back into the room, took the saucepan from her and put it on the table. 'Your supper?' he wanted to know, pleasantly.

She had retreated backwards until her back came against the table. 'How did you know where I was?'

'I went to East Sheen.' She saw him smile suddenly. 'Get your coat, we're going to have a meal and you shall tell me all about it.'

'No,' said Serena tartly, 'I won't!' and she didn't look at him, not when he was smiling like that.

'Just one room?' he asked gently, and strolled round examining it.

He edged his large person into the kitchenette and the shower-room too. 'All mod cons,' he observed, and wandered back to where she was still standing. Then he said gently, 'Get your coat, Serena.'

There was no point defying him—indeed, she didn't, in her heart, wish to. She got her coat from behind the curtain hung across one corner of the room which served as a wardrobe and put it on. 'My hair...' she said crossly. 'I've had no time...'

'You look very nice,' he observed, using the kind of voice he employed on his more nervous lady patients, and Serena was sufficiently soothed by it to go with him without another word.

Mrs Peck was in the hall, poking at a spider plant that took up all of one corner. The doctor paused deliberately by her. 'I'm taking Miss Proudfoot out to supper and shall see her safely back here at a reasonable hour, madam.'

'She could do with more meat on her bones,' observed Mrs Peck, and smiled just a little.

Serena gave a gasp of rage as he swept her out of the house. On the pavement she stood still. 'You seem to forget,' she told him icily, 'that I'm a woman of twenty-five, old enough to come and go as I like—if I wish to stay out until the small hours I shall do so!'

Which hadn't been quite what she had meant to say, only the words had come out wrongly.

'Now that,' said the doctor smoothly, 'sounds very promising. Do you like to dance the night away or shall we take a drive in the country? After a meal, of course.'

'That isn't what I meant and you know it. I—I think I won't come out with you, thank you all the same.' She made to turn round and make for the door, but his large hand on her arm stopped her.

'You're tired,' he said in a quite different voice. 'Come and have supper, and afterwards you shall vent your rage on me.'

She looked up at him and saw that he was smiling gently, and without being able to help it she smiled back.

'That's better.' He bent and kissed her cheek. 'How fierce you looked—I felt quite intimidated!'

She laughed then, and he tucked her hand in his arm and walked across to the car and stowed her into it, got in himself and drove away. She was too occupied thinking about the kiss to notice where they were going, but presently she saw that they were driving west through the city and presently through a number of side streets, quiet now after the day's bustle, until they reached Wigmore Street and then Wimpole Street and finally turned into a tree-lined street bordered by narrow houses. The doctor had kept up a placid conversation about nothing much as he drove, not allowing her the chance to ask questions, but when he stopped halfway down the street she asked, 'Why have we come here?'

'I live here.' He leaned over and undid her seatbelt and the door, then got out himself, bustled her across the narrow pavement and put a key in an elegant door. The hall was long and narrow, but unlike Primrose Bank it was carpeted and softly lighted and the staircase curved gracefully up one wall. As the doctor closed the door a short stout man with a fringe of grey hair came through a door at the back of the hall.

'Good evening, Bishop,' said the doctor. 'This is Miss Proudfoot, come to share my supper. Serena, Bishop and his wife look after me.'

He was taking off his car coat as he spoke and turned to help her out of hers. 'There's a cloakroom by the stairs if you want to tidy yourself. Bishop will show you. I'll pour us a drink.'

He spoke in matter-of-fact tones which made everything seem just as it should be. Serena followed Bishop and was bowed into a cloakroom which held everything required for the improvement of her appearance. As she inspected the result in the looking-glass she wondered how many other girls had prinked before it. 'And a good deal prettier than I am,' she told herself, 'and I can't think why he's doing this, unless he wants me to do an extra load of work...'

Whatever her host's motives were he didn't allow them to show. He ushered her into a charming sitting-room, furnished with a pleasing mixture of comfortable chairs and sofas and a scattering of what she guessed to be genuine Regency tables and cabinets, the whole nicely welded together by the soft lighting and plum-coloured velvet curtains which echoed the faded colours of the silky carpet under her feet.

The doctor pulled forward a chair and she stared round her, and then sat down near the brisk fire and accepted the drink he offered her, while he settled himself opposite to her.

It was then that she became aware of the dog sitting beside his chair. It peered at her through shaggy hair; it was of no great size and as far as she could judge of no known breed.

'Harley,' observed the doctor. 'He's shy of strangers. Do you like dogs?'

'Oh, yes! I had one——' she paused '—a long time ago.'

'Say hello, Harley,' said the doctor, and the dog came from beside his chair and walked sedately to her. She rubbed his ears and mumbled at him, and he stared at her with melting eyes.

'He's nice.' She looked him over. 'Where did you get him?'

'In the gutter in Harley Street. He was a puppy then, of course. I've had him for a couple of years.'

Harley went back to sit by his master, and a few minutes later Bishop came to tell them that dinner was served.

The dining-room was behind the sitting-room, a smallish room but still capable of seating eight people with ease round the oval table. The marquetry on the chairs and side table was quite beautiful, and the table was set with damask, silver and shining crystal. The meal, too, was as far removed from the saucepan of baked beans as it was possible to be: lettuce soup, chicken à la king with luscious roasted potatoes and braised chicory, and an apple pie and cream by way of pudding. Serena drank the wine the doctor poured for her; it was pale and dry and delicious, and she joined in his casual talk, for the moment happy. She hadn't known what to expect, but the evening was a delightful surprise.

They had their coffee in the sitting-room, and it wasn't until she had poured it that he said quietly, 'Now you shall tell me everything, Serena.'

However, when she just sat there, saying nothing, he went on, 'Your mother has married again, has she not?' and when she nodded, 'Suppose you start at the beginning and leave nothing out?'

She found herself telling him, slowly at first and doing her best to leave out the worst bits, but when she did that he took her back over it again until she had told him the whole. When she had finished he said nothing.

The silence lasted too long. Serena said quietly, 'I think I'd better go back, if you don't mind.'

He took no notice of this. 'Is there anything I can do to make things easier for you?' When she shook her head he asked, 'What about Christmas? Are you to go to Ludlow?'

She had been very honest with him—too honest, she reflected ruefully. Now she said in her quiet way, 'Oh, yes, that's all arranged. I have a few days' leave owing to me, so I shall be able to stay there for a while over the holidays.'

'How will you travel there? It is quite a long way.'

It was quite true; telling one lie only made it necessary to tell another and then another. 'Mr Harding will fetch me.'

He nodded. 'Good, and the leave will be convenient, for I shall be in Friesland.' He frowned. 'You are comfortable where you are? You can afford the rent?'

'Oh, yes, thank you. It's kind of you to ask.'

He became all at once remote. 'You must not forget that you are my secretary, Serena, and I am to a certain extent responsible for you.'

She took a gusty breath. 'That's nonsense!' She spoke heatedly. 'I must remind you once more that I am twenty-five and quite capable of looking after myself.' She let the breath out. 'I'm not one of your—your household.'

He said blandly, 'No, you have no need to remind me of that, Serena. I must apologise for interfering in your life. Have no fear—I'll not do so again. Now how about some fresh coffee?'

She got to her feet and he with her. 'I think I'd better go back. It's been very kind of you to give me supper—I enjoyed it.'

'A pleasure, Serena.' He had touched the bell by the fireplace and Bishop came in, and presently they were in the hall ready to leave. Serena bade Bishop goodbye, got into the car and was driven back to Park Street. The doctor talked about this and that as they went and she took care to answer him, and at the door of Primrose Bank she held out her hand.

'Thank you again—it was lovely. I'm sorry if I was rude.'

She couldn't see his face clearly for the street lighting was poor. He said, aloof once more, 'I didn't notice anything, and it is I who should thank you for a pleasant evening.' He took the key from her and opened the door and walked with her down the hall, waiting while she got her key, which he took from her and opened her own door. He switched on the light too, and when she had stepped past him, bade her a quiet goodnight.

Serena sat for a long time, heedless of the chill, thinking about the evening and Marc. She wasn't sure if she would be able to go on working for him, seeing him day after day, aware that over and above his concern for her he had no interest in her at all. He had been careful to point out to her only an hour or so ago that because she worked for him, he was responsible for her. On the other hand, never to see him again was something she couldn't even contemplate. 'And I told him all those fibs about Christmas,' she muttered, getting into bed at last. 'Not that he's likely to find that out—he'll be in Holland.' She had an unsettled night, waking every now and then to worry about Christmas.

Unnecessarily, as it turned out. There was a letter the next morning from Aunt Edith, sent on from East Sheen. The writer had met an old friend when she had been shopping in Devizes two days previously. The old friend lived in Ludlow and had mentioned in passing that an acquaintance of her husband's, a Mr Arthur Harding, was marrying again—a Mrs Proudfoot. Aunt Edith had failed to gain any further information about this and would like to know exactly the circumstances. 'It is unlikely,' she wrote in her large clear hand, 'that there are many Proudfoots around, and I was told that she was a widow. Be good enough, Serena, to write to me without delay. Your uncle and I are concerned as to your circumstances in the light of these recent events.' She was hers affectionately.

There was a PS too. They would be delighted to welcome her for Christmas if by any chance she happened to be free.

That evening, Serena sat down and answered the letter. It was a difficult letter to write, for Aunt Edith had never liked her mother. Serena, faithfully setting down the happenings of the last month or so, skimmed over the parts of which her aunt wouldn't approve, ending with an acceptance of her Christmas invitation.

A good start to the week, thought Serena, walking briskly to work the following Monday. There was a pile of work waiting on her desk and Mrs Dunn, her face as long as a fiddle, warned her that she might have to work late. 'I know Dr ter Feulen is in theatre, but there's some special case been added at the last minute—you won't get the notes before the late afternoon.'

She looked at Serena's rather pale face. 'You look under the weather. Not much chance to gallivant around if you're working for him, you know!'

It didn't matter for whom she worked, reflected Serena. She had, so far, had little chance to gallivant.

'I dare say he'll slow down once he's married,' went on Mrs Dunn, a remark which left Serena without breath.

Presently she managed, 'Oh, is he getting married?'

'He told his registrar so; said he might want to cut down on his work-load. I wonder who she is?' Mrs Dunn didn't expect an answer, for she went on, 'There's that pretty fair girl I saw him with once. Well, whoever she is, she'll do very well for herself; she'll be a baroness or whatever they call it in Holland, and she'll have everything she could possibly want. He's got a house too, somewhere near Wigmore Street— he's got consulting-rooms there, of course. I dare say he's got a home in Holland too.' Mrs Dunn paused. 'Oh, well, I don't suppose you're in the least interested. Why should you be? Settled in, have you?'

'Yes, thank you, Mrs Dunn. I'm very comfortable.'

Mrs Dunn went away, and Serena inserted the first of the sheets of paper into her typewriter. She made no attempt to start work, though. She sat quite still, her hands quiet in her lap, getting used to the idea that Marc was going to marry.

It was several days before she saw him again. He phoned several times with instructions and additions to his notes, but other than that he had nothing to say. Which, she told herself, was a very good thing.

On Tuesday she had a letter from her mother, full of the delights of her new home, the satisfaction of having someone to do the housework and cook, the delightful shops in Ludlow, and since the weather was so cold and wet they were leaving for Madeira several weeks earlier than they had first planned, which meant that Serena wouldn't be able to visit them until the New Year. Beyond a cursory remark about the splendid time Serena must be having, she had little else to say.

The letter from Aunt Edith was much more satisfactory. They were looking forward to seeing her at Christmas and she was to stay as long as she could. She didn't mention her mother at all, but reiterated that she would be as welcome as their own daughter, 'For,' wrote Aunt Edith, abandoning her stiffly correct writing, 'I loved your father very dearly.'

It was nice to be wanted. Serena slept soundly for the first time in weeks.

It was the following day that she acquired a cat. She had got home cold and wet, walking through a sleet which penetrated everything and stung her face. It had been a beastly day too; she had had to refer back to the doctor about several of his notes, and at the end of the afternoon, just as she was finishing for the day, he had sent up half a dozen letters he wanted typed at once.

Her room, despite the cheerful lampshades she had bought, looked miserably bare. She lighted the gas fire, took off her wet things and switched on the TV, then went to put on the kettle. The TV was making a strange thumping noise and she went to see what was wrong. However, it wasn't the TV—the thumps were coming from the garden—something was trying to get in. She turned the sound down and listened, her heart thumping too. Perhaps someone had left the garden gate unlocked... The noise came again and in the silence which followed a faint miaow.

Serena opened the door and then a small, very wet cat crawled in. It was so wet that it could be any colour, its fur plastered to a bony little body. She fetched a towel and picked up the small creature and dried it gently, warmed some milk and watched it lapping feebly.

'Well, I wanted a cat,' she told it, 'and now I've got it. Only I have to get you well fed and content again, don't I?'

She made a nest of a woolly scarf and laid the little beast before the fire, where presently it went to sleep, and when she had had her own supper she fed it again before it dropped off once more. When she went to bed she picked it up, scarf and all, and laid it carefully on the divan. It purred a little then and she stroked it very gently. 'You'll have to be alone all day,' she told it. 'But I'll leave food for you and we'll get organised tomorrow, and soon it will be Saturday, so I'll be here all day.'

She got up earlier than usual to see to the little cat, who, though still looking bedraggled, showed signs of taking an interest in its surroundings. It had a large breakfast, then got back on to the divan and curled up once more. Serena hoped it would stay like that until she got home.

The weather had worsened and by the afternoon it was snowing; a wet snow which turned to slush as soon as it had fallen. By the time she was ready to leave it was dark as well, and she debated whether to queue for a bus or walk. She would walk, she decided, poking her nose out of the entrance and getting it covered in snowflakes.

She pushed the door open wider and then had it taken from her grasp. 'I'm going your way, I'll give you a lift,' said the doctor, and swept her along with him across the forecourt and into his car.

When he stopped outside Primrose Bank she thanked him politely and made to get out, but his 'Stay where you are' stopped her. He got out and walked round the car to open her door and then go with her to the front door.

'There's really no need,' said Serena, and had the key taken from her hand.

Short of making a fuss and commotion in the hall there was no way of stopping him from going with her down the hall and through the door, to take the second key from her and open her room door. He stood aside for her to go in, and then followed her.

The cat was curled up in a rather dirty furry ball on the divan. It opened one eye as they went in, then closed it again.

The doctor shut the door behind him. 'You have a companion.' He went to look at the little beast and touched it with a gentle hand. 'Starved,' he commented. 'How did you come by it?'

'It tapped on the door yesterday evening. I hope it will be all right, it was very wet. I'm glad to have it.' She frowned. 'I can't go on calling it "it"...'

The doctor picked it up gently. 'A little lady cat,' he told her, 'and I think a very pretty one once she's fit again. While you find her some food, I'll put the kettle on. We can decide on a name while we have our tea.'

With the kitten tucked under one arm he saw to the kettle, put cups and saucers on a tray, found the milk and sugar and took biscuits from the cupboard. Serena, preparing bread and milk, thought of any number of things of a withering nature to say concerning people who invited themselves to tea, but somehow she didn't say them. The doctor had contrived to look like a man who needed his tea after a hard day's work, and she hadn't the heart to refuse him. Besides, having him there, making tea as though he did it every day of his life, which she very much doubted, made a bright patch of happiness in her sober life.

They drank their tea, decided to call the kitten Beauty and watched it climb laboriously on to the divan and fall instantly asleep. The doctor looked at his watch. 'I've an evening engagement.' He got to his feet and asked carelessly, 'All arranged for Christmas?'

'Yes, thank you.' She saw him to the door and stood by it watching him until he had disappeared through the door to the hall. He would be spending the evening with the girl he intended to marry. She washed up, tidied her kitchenette and sat down by the fire. There was a lot of evening left, and she had got clever at filling it after the first few evenings, when she had had her supper as soon as she came in and then had to fill in hours before bed. Presently she began a letter to Mevrouw Blom, who hadn't as yet been told about her mother's marriage.

It was still snowing in the morning. She attended to Beauty's needs, had her breakfast and, wrapped in her elderly coat and wearing her wellingtons, she left earlier than usual, intent on walking, as the buses would be packed. Her way took her through back streets and for part of the way alongside a small disused canal. The snow was blinding and she had her head tucked down to shield her face so that she saw very little, but as she reached the canal she heard a shout and stopped to look around her. There was no one in sight. It must have been someone in the houses on the other side of the street. Without delay she walked on, but at the second shout she stopped again, peering through the curtain of snow.

There was someone in the canal, floundering around, and as she looked disappearing beneath its murky surface. A head bobbed up—it was impossible to see whether it was man, woman, or child, and this time it wasn't a shout, more a water-filled gasp. Serena looked around her. There was no one to be seen and she doubted if she could get help from the houses across the street; quite a few of them were boarded up anyway. She gave a small sigh, got out of her coat, pulled off her wellingtons and lowered herself down the slippery bank into the dark brown and very cold water. She was a good swimmer and she had no doubt that she could haul whoever it was in the canal out of it. She gasped as she began to swim towards the bobbing head, and the icy water bit into her.

Marc, free until his appointments with private patients at noon, stood looking out of his sitting-room window. A very nasty day, he thought, and observed to Harley, 'I pity anyone forced to go out in this.' He glanced at his watch. Serena would be leaving for work shortly. He saw her in his mind's eye, arriving at the hospital looking like a small half-drowned mouse and soaked to the skin through that shabby coat...

A few minutes later he left his house with the
faithful Harley, Bishop's pleas that he should at least
eat his breakfast falling on deaf ears. He was probably
going on a wild goose chase, he pointed out to the
beast as they got into his car.

There was little point in going to Park Street. Serena
might have left already, but if he took the route from
the hospital which she had told him she used each
day, he might come upon her and at least drive her
the rest of the way. There was no sign of her as he
passed the hospital and followed the road she should
be taking by now. 'I'm a fool,' he told Harley. 'In all
probability she has managed to get on to a bus.'

He turned into the shabby street by the canal and
saw the small group of people halfway down it,
watching something in the water—more than something. Two heads bobbing up and down, making slow
difficult progress to the bank.

He had called the police and ambulance by the time
he reached the spot, and then he was out of the car,
his Burberry flung on its bonnet, and clambering down
the bank, before anyone there had time to see what
he was doing. The two in the water were a little nearer
now, and under the oil and filth he saw Serena's face
as he slid into its murky depths.

'Get yourself on to the bank,' he told her. 'I have
her now!' and Serena, numb with cold and tired to
death, did as she was bidden, only when she got to
the bank hauling herself out of the water was more
than she could manage. She heard Marc's voice giving
orders in a voice which expected obedience, and at
the same time she was given an efficient and undig-
nified boost from behind while several hands pulled
her on to the snowy path. She lay there, glad to be

alive, her teeth chattering, dripping icy water while she listened to a good deal of heaving and pushing and hard breathing close by. Someone laid a coat over her and she heard Marc say, 'Hold on, dear girl. She's alive, but only just.'

She slipped back into an icy limbo then until the ambulance and the police arrived, and very shortly after the blessed sound of Marc's calm voice. 'You're going in the ambulance, Serena. You need a check-up and a few hours to get warm again.'

'No, I'll go home... Will she be all right? The woman?'

'Thanks to you, yes, I think so.' She heard him chuckle. 'Next time pick someone your own size, Serena, she must weigh all of fifteen stone!'

She felt his hand on her hair. 'I'm filthy,' she muttered.

'Indeed you are.' He turned and looked down at her dirty face, pale under the mud, her hair in rats' tails, a small bruise over one eye, and she didn't see his smile.

She seemed to have lain there for hours, although in fact it was only minutes. The doctor politely picked her up and carried her to the ambulance, and she found herself lying on a stretcher beside the woman she had rescued. Marc was quite right, she was a very fat woman indeed, conscious now and complaining in a disjointed way. Serena closed her eyes and dozed off.

She was dreadfully sick in Casualty, and what with that and the dirt and mud and her clothes sticking wetly to her it all got a bit too much. She wept while Sister and a nurse undressed her and sponged her with warm water, and she was still weeping when the doctor, looking very clean and dressed in some miraculous way in a dry and elegant suit, came to look at her.

'Been sick?' he wanted to know cheerfully. 'Good, Sister, I'll take a look at her chest—are there any cuts and abrasions?'

She had been put into a theatre gown, and Sister lifted it here and there to show a few grazes and more bruises. 'Anti-tetanus to be on the safe side,' said the doctor, his stethoscope going from one end of her shoulder blades to the other. 'Sounds all right. She had better be warded for twenty-four hours.' He smiled down at her and, seeing her greenish face, handed her a bowl. Just in time!

'So sorry!' she gasped.

'No need. It's the best thing that could happen.' He patted her on the shoulder and went away.

'There,' said Sister, 'you'll probably be quite yourself by tomorrow.'

'He was in the water too,' said Serena.

'Yes, dear. How very fortunate that he happened to be passing and saw you both. You're a very brave girl.' She smiled kindly and passed the bowl again.

Sister was quite right—Serena felt perfectly well again by the next morning. She had been put in a room by herself and given delicious food and allowed to lie for ages in a hot bath and wash her hair. They had done that in Casualty, but only to get the worst of the debris out of it. She had woken early and started to worry about Beauty, but Night Sister, doing her last round, assured her that someone was looking after the kitten and that her coat and handbag had been collected and brought to the hospital. 'Someone will fetch you some clothes presently so that you can go home. You'll need a day or two before you go back to work.'

'The woman who was in the water—is she all right?'

'Doing nicely, dear. She'll be here for a few days, though. Now I'm going to get Nurse to bring you a cup of tea...'

Serena went to sleep again after her breakfast, and when she woke there were her clothes neatly piled on a chair by the bed. She could hear the distant clatter of plates, which meant dinnertime for the patients. It might be a good idea to get herself dressed before her dinner came, and then she supposed she would be allowed to go back to Park Street.

She was sitting quietly, dressed and ready for whatever was to happen next, when the doctor came in. Sister was with him, and they both stood and studied her for a moment. When he said quietly, 'Ready to go back, Serena?' she stood up and said just as quietly,

'Yes, thank you, sir,' and got her jacket. It wasn't really warm enough, but her coat, Sister had told her, had been sent to the cleaners. The doctor held it for her, waited while she thanked Sister for her care and ushered her out of the room.

In the corridor she stopped. 'I haven't had the chance to thank you for saving me—us—yesterday. I am very grateful.'

He nodded, and she wondered why he looked so aloof, and yet on their way to the entrance he was friendly enough.

'I'll get a taxi,' she told him, and held out a hand.

He took it and walked her through the door, opened the Bentley's door and popped her in. 'There's no need——' she began, and stopped at his curt, 'Don't argue, Serena.'

So she sat silently, but not for long. 'This isn't the way to Park Street,' she pointed out.

'You are to stay in my house for a few days. Mrs Bishop will look after you.'

'I can't, you know I can't! There's Beauty, she's all alone.'

'She's at my house. I fetched her yesterday when I went for your clothes.'

She looked at his stern profile. 'But there was no need . . .'

He didn't answer, and she became silent, feeling puzzled. There was something wrong, she knew that because she loved him, and she longed to ask him what it was, but she had no right to.

Bishop was hovering as they went into the house and Mrs Bishop, small and round and cosy, came from the kitchen to lead her upstairs to a pretty room, warm and carpeted and glowing with soft colours. 'Just you take off that jacket, miss, and come right down for your lunch,' said Mrs Bishop, and stood over her while she tidied her hair and powdered her small nose.

The doctor was waiting for her. They drank their sherry, making small talk until Bishop ushered them into the dining-room. He stayed in the room all the time so that Serena was quite unable to say anything she wanted to say. It was tiresome uttering platitudes and having them capped by her companion. She ventured a peep at him now and again. He looked inscrutable and, she fancied, angry. She wondered why.

She soon found out. They sat facing each other by the fire with Harley curled up on his master's feet and

Beauty on her lap. Serena poured the coffee and, still conscious of the silence between them, cast around for something to say. Much as she wanted to stay at Marc's house, she had decided during the last half-hour that it wouldn't do at all. He was being kind only because he felt it was his duty.

He put his cup down. 'I telephoned your mother, Serena.' His quiet voice sent a shiver down her back. 'You have been telling me a pack of lies.'

CHAPTER EIGHT

THERE was no point in denying it. Serena said, 'Yes, I know. I'm sorry.' A remark which was received with a mocking smile and a raised eyebrow so that she felt compelled to add, 'You're the very last person in this world I would lie to.'

A silly remark, she realised the moment she had uttered it, and justly deserving the doctor's look of cold disbelief. It would be better if she stayed silent. She stroked Beauty and looked at her shoes.

The doctor settled back in his chair. 'And now, suppose you tell me the truth of the matter, Serena.'

And, since there was really nothing else she could do about it, she did. 'You see,' she hastened to add when her tale was finished, 'it's all turned out very well, for I shall spend Christmas with Aunt Edith at Great Canning.'

His eye fell on the kitten. 'And Beauty?'

'Oh, I'll take her in a basket, I'm sure she'll be welcome.'

She was doing her best to behave naturally, but she could sense the barrier between them. Perhaps he would never trust her again, she thought gloomily, and it would serve her right, although at the time she had thought that she was doing the right thing. Overcome with sudden and ridiculous self-pity, she found herself wishing that she had drowned in the canal, then perhaps he would have been sorry. She had a clear picture of her lifeless form with him bending over her, full of remorse . . .

'Stop daydreaming, Serena, and listen to me. I shall be away for two days. You are to stay here, and Mrs Bishop will take care of you. By then you should be fit for work again. I will arrange for Bishop to drive you back to Park Street in two days' time so that you may start work on the following morning. If by some chance you don't feel that you have completely recovered be good enough to let Mrs Dunn know so that she can arrange for someone to take over from you.'

Serena said quickly, 'Is that what you would like, someone to work for you instead of me? I—I'd quite understand if you did.'

'Don't be ridiculous, Serena! I thought you a girl of common sense—you're talking like an irritable child.'

This was too much! She got to her feet, clutching Beauty. 'I think it would be best if I went to bed.'

It was disconcerting when he got up with a cheerful, 'Yes, a good idea. Your good sense will return after a sound night's sleep.'

He held the door for her and she went past him without looking up, muttering goodnight as she went.

Later, lying in her soft warm bed, she tried to be sensible and think what was best to be done. The dignified thing would be to find another job and go miles away where she would never see him again, but he might possibly guess at her reason, and that was unthinkable. Her love for him was a secret she was determined that no one would share, let alone guess. Common sense, gradually taking over again, urged her to go on just as she had been doing. She was, after all, just someone who worked for him, and in time he would forget the whole thing. Besides, he would have his wife to absorb his thoughts. Perhaps he was going to spend the two days with her. Serena began to imagine her; young and fair and beautiful, that went without saying, with cupboards full of lovely clothes and a delightful nature. She closed her eyes resolutely on tears and presently fell asleep.

No one could have been kinder than Mrs Bishop. Breakfast in bed, a gentle walk in the narrow garden at the back of the house, with Beauty darting to and fro, and then Bishop coming to call her indoors so that she could drink her coffee. The house was run on oiled wheels and Serena was treated like an honoured guest. Two days had never passed so quickly or so delightfully. At the end of the second one she collected her few possessions, and, with Beauty tucked under an arm, got into the Rover which Bishop had brought to the door, and was driven away with Mrs Bishop waving from the doorstep.

Park Street, still under a thin mantle of dirty snow, looked uninviting as Bishop drew up before Primrose Bank, got out, rang Mrs Peck's bell and held the door for Serena to get out. 'I'll see to your things, miss,' he assured her. 'You go ahead and open the doors if you will.'

Mrs Peck greeted her with a warmth she had hardly expected and followed her through the door to her own room. Serena unlocked the door, but made no attempt to go in. Someone had lit the gas fire and there were flowers on the table, a bowl of hyacinths on the bookshelf. There was even a tray laid for tea...

'Oh, how very kind! Mrs Peck, did you do all this? Thank you.'

'Well, yes, in a manner of speaking I did,' said Mrs Peck, and stood aside to allow Bishop to go past her with a large cardboard box.

He put it on the table. 'Mrs Bishop thought it might make things easier for you if you had your supper cooked ready for you.' He took a quick look round the room and thought how unsuitable it was for such a nice young lady. 'If there's anything I can do, miss, I'd be glad...'

'No, thank you, Bishop. But please tell Mrs Bishop how grateful I am for my supper, and you have both been so kind to me. Thank you again.'

'A pleasure, miss.' He cast a superior eye over Mrs Peck. 'I leave you in good hands, I have no doubt.'

He was not mistaken. Mrs Peck, despite her brusque manner, had a kind heart. Besides, Dr ter Feulen had given her more than enough for the flowers and all the extra gas she had used keeping the room warm, not to mention the tea and coffee and biscuits and so on she had been asked to purchase. She put the kettle on now and made the tea, observing gruffly that Serena was a heroine and make no mistake, and it was the least she could do. She then took herself off, looking embarrassed at showing so much sentiment.

Alone, Serena fed Beauty, who gobbled up her food and then settled before the fire, then sat down to drink her tea, and because she couldn't help but compare her surroundings with the comfort of the doctor's house she busied herself unpacking the box. There wasn't just supper in the form of a chicken pie, game chips and a winter salad, there were eggs, rolls, butter, cheese, a half-bottle of wine and a box of fruit.

'Well, look at all this,' declared Serena to a somnolent Beauty. 'How very kind of Mrs Bishop!' She began preparations for her supper, wondering if the housekeeper would tell the doctor what she had done and if he would mind. Not that it mattered—she had every intention of eating everything there and sampling the wine as well.

Someone had hung her coat behind the curtain, newly cleaned and pressed, and she was glad of it in the morning, for it was cold and although it was dry the sky was grey and threatening. She walked to work, racing past the canal as hard as she could go, not wanting to be reminded about it—if the woman hadn't fallen in and she hadn't gone in after her then there would have been no need for Marc to have rescued her and discovered about her mother. Oh well, it was over and done with now, and probably he had already put it out of his mind.

Which seemed to be the case, for beyond a preoccupied 'good morning' as she joined his team in Outpatients, he had nothing to say to her. Her day was busy, as usual, enlightened by several of the staff going out of their way to compliment her on her bravery, to all of whom she pointed out quite truthfully that if it hadn't been for Dr ter Feulen most probably she and the woman would have got into difficulties.

During the next few days it was as if he was avoiding her. Work appeared on her desk, set there by an unseen hand, sometimes with a scrawled note attached, and it wasn't until his last clinic of the week that Serena saw him again.

He stopped her as she was leaving the hospital. 'You have fully recovered?' he asked her austerely, and looked down his magnificent nose at her so that she wanted to turn and run away from him and his scornful look.

'Yes, thank you,' and since she hadn't had the chance to thank him properly, 'I'm very grateful to you and to Mr and Mrs Bishop, they were so kind...' She blushed then, for it sounded as though he hadn't been kind too. She added feebly, 'You too, of course, sir.'

His courteous, 'Thank you, Serena,' chilled her to the bone. Even if she had wanted to make amends she was given no chance, for he bade her a good evening in the same austere voice and stood there waiting for her to go on her way.

It wanted only a few weeks to Christmas, and everyone said that just for once it would be a white one, since it snowed on and off almost each day, although never enough for it to settle. Serena had had two postcards from her mother, both overflowing with the delights of sun and warmth and ending with a meaningless, 'See you soon,' which she didn't quite believe. She had had letters from Aunt Edith too, each one reiterating her pleasure at meeting Serena again for Christmas and making no objection to Beauty's presence then. Serena bought suitable presents and a cat basket, and in a fit of extravagance spent too much money on a pair of soft leather boots.

Life would have been dull if it hadn't been for the fact that she went to work each day in the hope of seeing Marc. Of course, on his clinic days she was there with the rest of his team, but beyond his usual civil and cool greeting he didn't speak to her unless it was something concerning her work. But that was better than nothing.

Watching him walk away after a businesslike session with his notes, she found it hard to believe that he was the same man who had taken her to see his family in Friesland. She must have annoyed him in some way, although she couldn't think how. Of course, he had ruined a suit going into the canal that morning, but he could certainly afford to buy a new one, and as far as she knew he was satisfied with her work. She worried about it quite a lot.

Christmas, as it always did each year, loomed within a day or two after weeks of being a vague festival ages away. The doctor had a clinic on Christmas Eve, and there was no suggestion that anyone should opt out. He did concede that the clinic should start an hour earlier than usual and close down at four o'clock so that anyone concerned would have a chance to get away to wherever they were going. Serena prudently packed her case on Christmas Eve morning, saw to her room, apprised Mrs Peck of her absence for a couple of days, and went to work in good time. She was left alone in the morning so that her desk was cleared by the time the afternoon clinic started, and since it was so near Christmas there weren't as many patients as usual. If the doctor had a spark of pity in him he would let her off the typing until she got back after Christmas . . .

The festive season appeared to leave him unmoved. The clinic wound its slow way through the afternoon and there were still two patients to see at four o'clock. Staff Nurse had been allowed to go because she was catching a train to York, but Sister was still there and so were the registrar and his houseman as well as two students. Serena, in her corner, sharpened another pencil and tried not to feel impatient. She hadn't the time to get her ticket first, and if the queue at the booking office was very long she would miss her train and the next one as well. Beyond that she didn't dare to think. The last patient went at quarter to five and the process of tidying up around the doctor, still writing busily at his desk, began.

Serena, resigned and cross, asked woodenly, 'When would you like these notes, sir?'

'When you return to work, will do, Serena.' He glanced up briefly. 'Are you going to your aunt's by train?'

'Yes.'

'I have to go to Bristol tonight. Be ready by six o'clock and I'll drop you off on my way. Have you got your train ticket?'

'No!' She put a great deal of ill temper into the word.

'Good. You will have little chance of getting a train this evening without one; by the time you have bought it the last train will have left.'

'What a good idea, sir,' sighed Sister kindly. 'What luck for you, Serena! Run along quickly and get home and get your things so you don't keep the doctor waiting.'

Serena looked at the faces smiling at her, all except the doctor's, of course. They all had something to say and they all urged her to get home fast as she could. There was really nothing she could do about it, although she longed to refuse him. She said quite meekly, 'Thank you, sir, that is very kind of you.' She glanced at him and saw his faintly mocking smile, and wished she hadn't spoken. She gathered her things together, wished everyone a happy Christmas and hurried away to lock the notes in her desk and drag on her coat and race out of the hospital. Be ready by six o'clock, he had said in his arbitrary way, which gave her a little less than an hour.

She would have been ready for him when he knocked on her door, but Beauty had decided right at the last minute that a cat basket was the very last place in which she wished to be. She had retreated behind the little cooking stove and no amount of blandishments would budge her.

The doctor breezed in with, 'Not ready?' uttered in a tone which implied only too clearly that he hadn't expected her to be anyway.

'I'm quite ready,' said Serena crossly, 'but Beauty doesn't like her basket.'

It was really most annoying when he called, 'Puss, puss!' in a beguiling voice, and Beauty scampered out at once and made no fuss at all when he picked her up and popped her into the basket.

'You see?' he said smugly.

'Pooh!' said Serena pettishly, and then, 'I could have gone by train...'

'So you could, provided you had caught Beauty in time, found a taxi, and bought a ticket before the last train had left.'

Which was true enough.

Traffic was light, as most people who were going away for Christmas had long since gone. The doctor went west out of the city, got on to the motorway and then the A303. The journey was just over a hundred miles, and a little over two hours later he was slowing down at the approach to Great Canning. During that time he had been a delightful companion, carrying on a vague conversation which was about nothing at all and never once showing the least interest in herself.

Serena, sitting quietly beside him, wasn't sure whether to be pleased about it or not.

'I should think the vicarage is close to the church,' she offered uncertainly as they drove into the main street and she glimpsed its tall spire, and sure enough just past the church a pleasant old house, its windows lighted, came into view. It stood back from the road with its gate, opening on to a short drive, wide open.

The doctor stopped before the door and she said quickly, 'You'll come in? My aunt and uncle will want to meet you if you can spare the time.'

'I shall be delighted. At what time did they expect you?'

'Well, about ten o'clock. I was going to get a taxi from Devizes...'

'In that case, if you'd like to ring the doorbell I'll collect your case and Beauty.'

Aunt Edith came to the door. She looked as stiff and proper as the letters she wrote, but her voice was warmly welcoming. 'Serena, my dear child.' She offered a cheek for Serena to kiss. 'You're early—you caught an earlier train?'

She caught sight of the doctor then, and Serena said, 'This is Dr ter Feulen, who very kindly gave me a lift. He has to go to Bristol.'

Her aunt shook hands and peered at him through her spectacles. 'How very kind! Do come in. You will have time for a cup of tea or coffee?'

He assured her gravely that he had, put the case down in the hall and handed Beauty in her basket to Serena.

Her aunt led the way into the sitting-room, comfortable and a little shabby but bright with flowers and a brisk fire. She said, slightly flustered, 'Do take off your coats, I'll put them in the hall. You must forgive me, I didn't expect... That is, I had no idea you had a young man, Serena.'

Serena went a delicate shade of pink and the doctor, watching her, smiled. He said nothing, and it was left to her to answer as best she could.

'Not my young man, Aunt Edith,' she said in what she hoped was a perfectly natural voice. 'Dr ter Feulen is a consultant at the Royal Hospital, and I do his typing. He—he just happened to be coming this way, and since I had Beauty and the trains are all over the place and I hadn't got my ticket...' She stopped, aware that she was making too much of the whole thing.

'A perfectly natural mistake,' said the doctor smoothly. 'Serena is my right hand.'

Aunt Edith waved them to chairs and sat down herself. 'You're not a married man?' she wanted to know.

If the doctor was taken aback at this remark he gave no sign. 'Not at the moment, though I plan to marry very shortly.'

Aunt Edith nodded her head. 'Doctors should be married men,' she observed, 'just as clergy should.' She broke off as the door opened and her husband came in.

'I heard voices,' he said, and smiled at the room's occupants. 'I see that Serena has arrived—how delightful! When I saw you last, my dear, you were a very little girl.' He kissed her in an absent-minded fashion and turned to the doctor, who had got to his feet. 'And you're her young man?'

'That's what I thought,' said Aunt Edith, 'but he's not. This is Dr ter Feulen from the hospital where Serena works, and he has given her a lift.'

'How very kind.' He offered a hand. 'You'll stay the night?'

'I regret I can't do that—I have appointments this evening...'

'In Bristol,' said Serena, just to remind him.

'I'll get the coffee,' observed her aunt, and shook her head at Serena's offer of help, leaving her to sit there while the two gentlemen started an absorbing conversation about medieval churches. Serena listened to Marc giving as good as he got, tossing hagioscopes, dossal curtains and sedilia into the discussion and countering her uncle's parclose screens, parvis stairs and naves with knowledgeable ease.

Serena sat there listening to these gems of architectural knowledge, her mouth slightly open, until the doctor caught her eye. 'Your uncle has a church to be proud of,' he told her. 'Twelfth-century, and with such a history.'

'I haven't been here since I was a little girl,' answered Serena coldly, 'and I can't remember the church.'

'Ah, well,' his voice held kind indulgence, 'you will have an opportunity to refresh your memory.'

Her mumbled reply was overlooked as her aunt returned with the coffee-tray and a plate of mince pies.

The doctor had two cups of coffee and several mince pies before he got to his feet and expressed his thanks and good wishes for a happy Christmas. Then he said that he should be on his way. He shook hands with her aunt and uncle and they all went into the hall to see him off. His coat on and ready to go, he paused by the open door and before Serena could move out of his reach had kissed her. 'I shall be here at eight o'clock on Boxing Day,' he told her, and got into the car and drove away.

Her uncle closed the door and Aunt Edith said, 'A very nice man, he must be splendid to work for,' and then as they all went back into the sitting-room, 'I dare say it's the usual thing to kiss in modern times. We're a little out of date here.'

Serena, all the good sense knocked out of her, pulled herself together. 'It's because it's Christmas,' she offered, and was relieved to see that her companions accepted her explanation. Only it wasn't one she could accept herself. There was really no reason for Marc to kiss her with such—she hesitated for a word—enthusiasm seemed to fit. But whatever the reason, she had enjoyed it.

Marc, driving back the way he had come, bent on getting to the airfield where his chartered plane was waiting, had enjoyed it too. It was a pity he couldn't have stayed on to see how Serena had reacted.

The airfield, some miles outside London, was an hour and a half's drive, the plane was waiting for him, and he transferred himself and his luggage without loss of time, leaving the Bentley to be garaged until he returned.

'Should be a good trip,' the pilot told him. 'You'll be there by midnight—anyone to meet you at Leeuwarden?'

'Yes. Do you fly back here tonight?'

The man grinned. 'I've got a wife and kids. But I'll be there on Boxing Day—don't give yourself much of a break, do you?'

'No—but it's Christmas, worth making the effort.'

'I bet you need it—a doctor, aren't you? It's in the book. Nod off if you've a fancy to do that—been hard at it all day, have you?'

'You could say that, and I think I'll take your advice.' The doctor closed his eyes, but he didn't go to sleep. He thought about Serena.

She was sitting between her aunt and uncle, eating her supper. No one said anything more about Marc, which disappointed her, for she longed to talk about him, but she was questioned closely about her mother and her new husband and the circumstances leading to Serena having to find herself somewhere to live.

'It's not my business to criticise,' said Aunt Edith, doing just that, 'but surely there was sufficient money from the sale of your father's house to allow you to buy a small flat. As you know, child, your mother and I never got on, and if I speak plainly you must forgive me. I can only hope that you are comfortably situated. Park Street sounds pleasant enough.' Her eye fell on Beauty, sitting as good as gold on the carpet. 'And having that dear little kitten for company must make your flat homelike.'

Serena agreed, having no wish to disillusion her companions about the pleasantness of Park Street or the homely sphere of her room. They were dears, their view of life quite different from hers, but they were anxious to make her happy. Uncle Edgar, tall and thin and stooping, had accepted her as well as Aunt Edith.

They went back to the sitting-room after they had helped Mrs Hiscock, the family help, to clear the table, and presently Aunt Edith suggested that Serena might like to go to bed. 'For you will want to go to church with me in the morning. Your uncle will have the midnight service later, but you must be too tired for that.'

'I'd like to come with you, if I may. It's the nicest service of 'Christmas, and I'm not a bit tired.'

It was the start of a lovely Christmas. They came back at one o'clock in the morning to hot cocoa and more mince pies, and Serena slept dreamlessly in the nice old room with the creaking floorboards and a fearful draught from its old warped windows. The bed was cosy and someone had put a hot-water bottle in it.

Uncle Edgar had to take the early morning service, and she got up to help her aunt tidy the house before he came back for his breakfast, since Mrs Hiscock wouldn't be coming. They went to church again for matins and had their Christmas dinner at three o'clock, at which time they opened their presents. Uncle Edgar had given her a book token and Aunt Edith had knitted her a thick cardigan. She was glad that she had splashed out on the presents she had bought for them—a pretty shawl for her aunt and a combined diary and notebook for her uncle. They pulled crackers, ate their turkey and Christmas pudding and drank a glass of port the vicar produced, before washing up and then going to sit round the fire comfortably doing nothing. Serena, who had been dreading Christmas, discovered that she was enjoying herself, and sitting there with her somnolent companions on either side of the fireplace, she had the leisure to think about Marc. She didn't know about Christmas in Holland, but surely his family would have gathered together. But he had gone to Bristol. She allowed her thoughts to become exaggerated, thinking of him in the bosom of some family whose daughter he was going to marry. It was a relief when her aunt suggested that they might have a cup of tea.

Aunt Edith, never one to beat about the bush, wanted to know what Serena's mother had sent her for Christmas.

'Well,' said Serena, 'I rather think she may have forgotten that it's Christmas. You see, it's more or less summer there, isn't it, so there won't be anything to remind her...'

Aunt Edith snorted in a well-bred fashion. 'It is December the twenty-fifth all over the world,' she pointed out severely, ignoring her husband's gentle remarks about latitude and longitude and differences in time.

'I expect there will be something when I get back,' said Serena, anxious to avoid the penetrating questions her aunt fired at her.

Aunt Edith had a thirst for knowledge. 'This nice doctor who gave you a lift here—do you know him well? You work for him, so presumably you must have close contact with him?'

'Well, in a way, yes. But I quite often don't see him for several days—he leaves work for me, and little notes, and of course the clinics happen fairly often, and then I just sit and take shorthand notes about the patients, and afterwards I type them and he signs them.' She paused. 'He is really very nice to work for.'

Her voice had taken on a warmth she hadn't realised. Her aunt gave her a sharp look and gave another prod in search of more information.

'You are fortunate, Serena. I dare say he gives you a lift home if you're late?'

Serena fell into the trap without thinking. 'Oh, yes, and when he got me out of the canal he took me to his home and his housekeeper looked after me—she was so kind, even though he wasn't there, and when he got back he drove me back to Park Street.'

Aunt Edith digested this rapidly. 'You fell into the canal?'

'Well, no, not quite—you see, there was a woman who had fallen in—and I went to help, and he got us both out.'

Aunt Edith knew when to stop. 'How very fortunate that he was at hand,' she commented, and went on vaguely, 'London must be such a busy place. It is years since we were there.'

So they talked about that, and the doctor wasn't mentioned again.

Boxing Day—St Stephen's Day—had its quota of church services, but her aunt suggested that a good walk would do Serena more good than going to church, and she was packed off in the kindest way possible to go to Roundway Down, the scene of the Royalist victory over the Roundheads in the middle of the seventeenth century. It was a mile away from the village, and Serena enjoyed the walk there and back. It was a bleak day, but even in midwinter the country looked beautiful in a quiet, sleepy way.

It was later that day, after they had washed up lunch and gone to sit by the fire in the sitting-room while her uncle went to his study, that Aunt Edith said suddenly, 'You're not happy, are you, Serena? Were you upset when your mother married again?'

'Yes, I think I was, but I don't think I was surprised. You see, she's the kind of person who needs someone to look after her...'

'Something which you were doing!' Her aunt's voice was tart.

'Yes, but you see, she was alone all day. I didn't get home until about six o'clock . . .'

'She had all day, then, to look after the house and to shop and cook.'

'We had a nice maid when Father was alive, and he did a lot . . .'

'And you carried on,' observed Aunt Edith drily. 'Where did your mother meet this Mr Harding?'

'In Amsterdam.' Serena paused and her aunt said, 'Yes? Hadn't you better tell me all about it, my dear? There is something making you unhappy, and to talk about it may help. I dare say we shan't see each other for a while, which makes it even easier.' Her rather stern face relaxed into a smile. 'It isn't just your mother, is it?'

'No, but it's all a bit—a bit silly . . .'

'Love is never silly,' said Aunt Edith. 'Suppose you start at the beginning, dear?'

It was such a relief to talk. Once she had started Serena couldn't stop, and somehow Marc crept into everything she said. She did her best to keep to her usual matter-of-fact manner, but she got to the bit where her aunt had mistaken him for her young man and she stopped because she wanted to cry, and that wouldn't do at all.

'You love him very much, don't you, dear?' said her aunt gently.

It was no use. Two tears trickled their slow way down Serena's cheeks. 'Oh, yes! What am I going to do?'

She got up and cast herself down beside her aunt's chair, and that lady put her arms round her. 'Have a good cry, child,' she advised. 'It will clear your head.'

Serena lifted a weeping face. 'But he'll be here...'

'He said eight o'clock, and it's barely four o'clock. Cry all you want, Serena, and when he comes meet him with a cheerful face.'

She allowed Serena to sob and sniff and presently asked, 'Does he like you, dear?'

Serena's voice came muffled from her aunt's lap. 'I don't know. He looks down his nose at me.'

A childish remark which made her aunt smile faintly. 'I don't know a great deal about such matters and I hesitate to give advice...' She broke off as the door opened and her husband, followed by the doctor, came in.

The vicar disappeared at once; he had heard the car and opened the door before the bell could be rung and ushered their visitor into the sitting-room, unaware of anything amiss. The fewer people there the better, he decided. Besides, Edith was so good at dealing with awkward situations.

So was Marc. He took in the situation at a glance, advanced to the room's occupants and said disarmingly, 'I must apologise, I'm so much earlier than I intended.' He didn't appear to see Serena, although he removed the sopping wisp she was clutching and substituted a large and very white handkerchief from his pocket. 'The vicar admitted me, but really I should have given you some warning.'

Aunt Edith rose to the occasion. 'We are delighted to see you, and you have no need to apologise—indeed, I am delighted, because now you can have supper before you leave. Cold turkey hangs heavy on one's hands after a day or so—you can help us to eat it up.' She patted Serena's shoulder. 'And you run along, my dear, and take a couple of aspirins before that headache gets any worse.' And as Serena got to her feet, 'She's been such a comfort to us, and such splendid company.'

'Hello,' said Serena, forced at last to say something. She had mopped her face more or less dry and she knew she looked just about as awful as any girl could look, so she avoided looking at him. She had cried herself to a standstill and she didn't care what she looked like. She added with a rather watery snap, 'I didn't expect you just yet.'

To all of which he said nothing, only opened the door for her and then came to sit down at Aunt Edith's invitation.

'Did you have a pleasant time in Bristol?' asked Aunt Edith.

'I've been in Holland at my home.' He smiled a little. 'I wanted to drive Serena here and I had to have an excuse—Bristol seemed a suitable one.'

'Are you sorry for Serena?' asked Aunt Edith bluntly.

'Certainly not, if by that you mean that I pity her. She is a resourceful girl and far too independent. She is, if I might put it rather clumsily, a hard nut to crack.'

Aunt Edith chuckled. 'But you'll crack it?'

'Certainly.' They smiled at each other in perfect understanding as Serena, nicely made up and neat about the head, her beaky nose still pink, came back into the room.

CHAPTER NINE

THE doctor got to his feet with the unselfconscious good manners which Aunt Edith entirely approved of. 'Your aunt has been telling me that Beauty has behaved beautifully and has everyone in the house a slave.'

A remark which included Serena immediately in the conversation, and since she had to make some sort of a reply it gave her no chance to feel awkward. Presently the vicar joined them and the two ladies went away to get the tea.

'Sandwiches,' decided Aunt Edith in the kitchen. 'Your uncle likes Gentleman's Relish and I dare say Dr ter Feulen does too. Cut the bread, will you, dear? I'll warm up some mince pies.'

She swiftly bustled round the kitchen carrying on a monologue about supper. 'Cold turkey and the ham, and I'll put some potatoes in the Aga to bake. Perhaps you would make a salad, dear? Do you suppose biscuits and cheese would do, or should I do something with the rest of the pudding?'

'Cheese and biscuits. Aunt Edith, did he notice? I must have looked a perfect fright!'

'Men aren't observant,' declared Aunt Edith untruthfully, adding silently, 'Only when they want to be,' and Serena sighed thankfully.

'It was kind of you to say I had a headache.'

Her aunt arranged cake on the plate. 'Your uncle doesn't condone lies, but I felt justified on this occasion, because a bout of weeping always brings on a severe headache.'

'Did he say if he'd had a good Christmas?'

'Yes, he had had a splendid time, he told me, but far too short.'

'Well, I expect so,' said Serena sadly, imagining him bidding an unwilling farewell to whoever it was in Bristol. 'It's clinic day tomorrow too.'

'You will be hard at work again, child. But you must promise me that you will come and see us soon. You will be more than ever welcome, you and Beauty.' She cast an eye over the sandwiches. 'Do you suppose we should cut the crusts off? I can put them out for the birds. Will you feed Beauty before you go? It will be late for her supper by the time you get back.'

They bore the tea-tray back to the sitting-room and there was a mild shuffling of chairs, handing of plates and teacups before everyone had settled down.

'Tea around the fire is so pleasant,' observed the vicar, 'one of the compensations of winter. You enjoyed your Christmas?'

'Very much,' declared the doctor, and avoided Aunt Edith's eye. 'Do you take evensong this evening?'

'Indeed, yes.' The good man gave the doctor a faintly enquiring look.

'Then may I come along too?'

'A pleasure—and it will give the ladies the opportunity to get our supper ready.'

That night, tucked up in her divan bed, back in her flatlet, Serena reviewed the evening. They had had supper, a splendid meal she and her aunt had contrived, and they had sat over it, the conversation lively, amusing and occasionally so well informed that she hadn't been sure what they were talking about, and when at last they had made their farewells they had driven back to Park Street, and so calm and casual had been Marc's manner that she had forgotten about her disgraceful bout of weeping and had enjoyed every minute of the journey. At Primrose Bank he had carried her case and Beauty into her room, switched on all the lights, lighted the gas fire, tested the locks on the doors and windows and wished her a friendly goodnight, adding a reminder that the morning's clinic would be a heavy one.

It had been midnight by then, and she had made herself a warm drink, fed a sleepy kitten and tumbled into bed. The Christmas she had been dreading had turned out to be one of the nicest she could remember, with the added bonus of Marc's company. She hugged that thought to her. There was so much about him that she loved even when he was at his most annoying.

She curled up around her hot-water bottle and Beauty curled up with her. 'All the same,' said Serena to herself, 'I shall have to go away, you know; he's not a fool, and sooner or later he's going to guess, and I couldn't bear it if he pitied me. Perhaps we might go nearer to Aunt Edith.'

Beauty stopped purring for a moment to miaow sleepily. 'You're not much help,' said Serena, and went to sleep herself.

The day began badly; she overslept, laddered her tights and hadn't the time to do her face properly, which, coupled with the cold grey morning, did nothing for her looks. The buses were few and far between and full of cross people having to go to work when they wanted to stay at home. When she got to the hospital she had to race up and down forbidden stairs and through corridors sacrosanct to the use of the consultants and their like. There was no one to see her, which was a good thing. She gained the doctor's clinic with moments to spare, rather out of breath and very conscious of the ladder, but she wished everyone a good morning and tried not to mind when the doctor looked up from his desk and glanced at her as though she wasn't there.

No one was feeling particularly good-natured. The thought that outside the hospital there would be untold thousands still enjoying a prolonged Christmas break soured those working within it, and the patients weren't best pleased at having to give up what might have been a nice lie-in to attend the clinic.

The doctor appeared impervious to the peevishness of his patients, and those working with him knew better than to voice their own ill humour. In any case, they liked him as much as they respected the way he worked.

The clinic over, Serena went off to her lunch, long overdue, and began work on the notes, and then without pause started on those she hadn't typed on Christmas Eve. Underneath those was a folder—another few pages of the book. It would have to wait until the next day; it had gone five o'clock a long time ago, and the quicker she went home and got the rest of the day over the better.

She was left in peace for the next few days. The doctor was catching up on ward rounds, private patients and theatre work, and when the next clinic—an afternoon one—came round everyone was back to normal. Christmas was over for another year and the talk was of New Year.

She was free on New Year's Day; she got home the evening before, looking forward to a lazy day in Beauty's company. She had hardly set eyes on Marc, but that didn't stop her thinking about him all the time. She was more than ever determined to find a job away from London, for she could see no future for herself; she had thought just once or twice that he liked her and, indeed, he had been friendly and always kind, but since Christmas he had retreated behind his bland face and only spoken to her when it was necessary. It was silly to go on like that, she told herself, and she would have to do something...

She fed Beauty, poked her nose into her tiny food cupboard and decided on soup out of a tin and scrambled eggs for supper, and even decided to have a shower before she ate.

Dressing-gowned, her hair loose around her shoulders, she was weighing the merits of cream of tomato against chicken noodle soup when someone knocked on her door. She frowned. It was barely eight o'clock and Mrs Peck had told her that the nurses upstairs were all going to a party and the elderly couple on the top floor had gone to their daughter's for the New Year. It could, of course, be Mrs Peck wanting a gossip. Serena went to the door as the knock was repeated.

'Mrs Peck?'

The unmistakable deep voice of the doctor answered her. 'Certainly not. Be good enough to open the door, Serena.'

'Well, I don't think I can—I'm in my dressing-gown, getting my supper.'

'Much too early for supper—and recollect that I have four sisters, all of whom I have seen in dressing-gowns.'

He sounded like a big brother too. She opened the door.

He looked at the tins of soup and his lip curled. 'I thought we might celebrate the New Year together. Mrs Bishop has prepared a splendid meal which it would be sinful to eat alone.'

'I'm just going——' began Serena.

'Ah, yes, I can see that. Cream of tomato soup in a tin.' He appeared not to look at her. 'I'll wait outside. Let me have Beauty in her basket and then get some clothes on—ten minutes long enough?'

'But I don't...'

He did look at her then. He smiled too, although he said nothing, and she said weakly, 'All right. Do I have to dress up?'

'Wear that grey thing, and for heaven's sake put on a thick coat. It's freezing outside.'

He had captured Beauty and was urging her gently into her basket.

'Ten minutes,' he reminded her as he closed the door gently behind him.

She flew into her clothes, did her face with care, arranged her hair in its usual neat bun and got into her coat. It took only a few moments to turn out the fire, check the windows and door and switch off the lights, then lock the door behind her.

Marc got out of the car as she left the house, bundled her smartly into the car, got in himself, and drove off. Serena, turning her head to make sure that Beauty was safe on the back seat, encountered Harley's melting gaze. He thumped his tail in greeting and she said, 'How nice to see you again, Harley.' It crossed her mind that Marc must surely have friends with whom he might spend his New Year's Eve, which thought naturally compelled her to ask, 'You're not having a party, are you?'

'No, Serena, just you and I,' and since there was a lot of traffic she forbore from saying anything else for fear of distracting his attention.

Bishop opened the door as they got out of the car and she was hurried into the warmth of the hall, where Bishop took her coat, undid Beauty's basket and handed her over very gently before opening the sitting-room door.

The room welcomed her; it was warm and softly lighted and there was a bright fire burning in the hearth. There was music too, something quiet and soothing.

'Delius?' asked Serena, taking the easy chair Marc offered her and settling Beauty on her lap.

'Very restful.' The doctor sat down in his chair with the faithful Harley at his feet and began a meandering conversation about classical music, and Serena, who had been feeling rather uncertain about everything, relaxed. Presently he got up, gave her a drink and got himself one, and edged the conversation round to her own affairs. He did it very carefully and she wasn't aware of it at first. But in the middle of explaining exactly why it wasn't possible for her to go to Ludlow, she realised that he had been egging her on to tell him a deal more than she had ever intended.

She finished what she was saying rather lamely and sat twiddling her thumbs round the glass in her hand. 'Why do you want to know about me?' she asked. 'Anyway, you already know as much as you need.'

She encountered his quizzical gaze and blushed. 'That
was awfully rude; I didn't mean it quite like that. What
I meant was that you must have a great many other
things to be interested in...' She put the glass down
on the lamp table by her chair. 'I don't think I should
have had that sherry—I didn't have time for any
lunch...'

'Mrs Bishop will be delighted to hear that; you will
do full justice to dinner.'

As if he had been waiting for his cue, Bishop came
to tell them that they were served. 'I'll take the little
cat, miss, and Mrs Bishop will give her a meal when
she feeds Harley.'

The meal was superb. Mrs Bishop, who on various
previous occasions had been forced to produce
nouvelle cuisine, only to have half of it uneaten by
the sylphlike ladies who had come to dine with the
doctor, allowed herself the pleasure of making rich
sauces, dishing up lobster thermidor, vegetables in
butter and preceding these with a rich artichoke soup
laced with cream, and by way of afters a trifle, loaded
with calories. 'Because,' she explained to Bishop, 'that
nice Miss Proudfoot enjoys good food, and another
pound or two won't spoil that nice figure of hers.'

The doctor must have been of the same opinion,
for he pressed Serena to second helpings and passed
her a dish of *petits fours* with the coffee.

Serena, who hadn't been looking forward to the
New Year in the least, found herself enjoying her
evening. Dinner had been splendid, but she would
have been just as happy without it since she had Marc
for company.

They hadn't hurried over their meal, and it was after
ten o'clock when they went back to sit by the fire with

Harley and Beauty, nicely full, sitting side by side before it.

The conversation until now had been pleasantly general and they had fallen into a friendly silence, to be broken by the doctor.

'What do you wish for the New Year, Serena?' he asked.

She stared at him, collecting wool-gathering thoughts in order to make a sensible reply. 'Oh, well— I don't know.'

It was the best she could manage at a moment's notice. She could, of course, tell him that she wished very much to stay with him for the rest of their lives; she wondered what he would say...

'You must have some idea,' he prompted gently. 'To travel, perhaps, come into a fortune, get married?' He was smiling at her in a way to make her heart turn over. She looked away and the thought came into her head that this was an opportunity to tell him that she would like to go away—right away from London, for to her that seemed the most sensible thing to do. She couldn't stay, seeing him continuously and loving him a little more each day and finally dwindling into a lovelorn old maid. He was going to marry. She wondered for the hundredth time who the girl was. Dutch, of course...

She spoke in a rush and rather too loudly. 'Yes, there is something I want to do more than anything else—leave London and the hospital and go miles away to some small town—perhaps near Aunt Edith. I want to start again, have another future. There must be something round the corner...'

If Marc was surprised nothing of it showed on his face. He said slowly, 'Do you suppose you're so anxious to see what is round the corner that you're missing something? You can be so busy looking for the moon that you miss the moonlight.'

'Oh, pooh!' said Serena, quite forgetting her manners. 'I'm all for carving a career.'

'Starting at the New Year?'

'Yes.' She bent over Beauty so that she didn't need to look at him, which was a good thing, because the thoughtful calculation on his face might have warned her. She was already sorry that she had been so vehement and was casting around for some means of putting things right when Bishop came in, bearing champagne in an ice-bucket.

Then she had no more chance, for it was almost midnight and Bishop, with Mrs Bishop in tow, joined them, ready for the first stroke of Big Ben. He timed the opening of the champagne to a nicety. They were raising their glasses as the New Year was ushered in, exchanging greetings and good wishes, and when the Bishops had gone again Serena said feverishly, 'That was lovely. Thank you for a lovely evening. I must go back...'

Marc showed no sign of having heard her. He was sitting in his chair looking comfortably relaxed. He said, 'You want to start again? You were serious, Serena?'

She bit off the 'No' she wanted to utter. 'Of course,' she told him.

'In that case, let me make things easier for you. You can leave at the end of the week—nothing could be easier. I am going on holiday for a couple of weeks and someone can be found to replace you during that time. Let me have your resignation in writing when you come to work and I'll arrange things for you.'

It was a shock, like taking a step that wasn't there. Serena gaped at him while she sought for words.

'You mean I can leave—just like that?'

He nodded, smiling.

'Haven't I been satisfactory?' A silly question, but she had to know.

'Quite satisfactory,' he told her seriously, 'very nearly as good as Muriel.'

'I should like to go home. It's been a lovely evening, but it's late.'

He made some sort of civil remark, the kind any good host might make, and Bishop was summoned to get her coat. Presently she was sitting beside Marc with Harley and Beauty in the back of the car, being driven back to Park Street.

There were people on the streets, celebrating, but not much traffic, and Serena, desirous of keeping her end up at all costs, made small talk, so intent on doing so that she failed to notice that her companion, beyond the odd murmured grunt, had almost nothing to say.

At Primrose Bank he slid to a silent halt, got out and opened her door, lifted Beauty from the back seat and, leaving Harley to guard the car, crossed the pavement to the door. Serena, her key clutched in her hand, offered the other one. 'Thank you very much,' she said politely, 'and it was a lovely dinner. Mrs Bishop is a gem, isn't she? Your—your wife will be delighted to have her.'

He ignored her hand, took the key from the other one and opened the door. 'They will get on very well,' he observed, and at once stood aside to let her pass him. He opened her room door too, switched on the light, inspected the windows and curtains as he always did, and put Beauty's basket down before the fire, stooping to light it.

'Thank you very much,' said Serena, and wished she could think of something else to say.

He crossed the room to stand before her. He didn't speak, but took her in his arms and kissed her, thoroughly and without haste.

'Do you still want to go away?' he asked her.

Serena found her voice, rather a small one, for she was shaken to her very bones. It would be so easy to say no, but she drew back a little and he let her go at once.

'Yes, yes, I do.'

'Will you tell me why? Don't you think you should do that?'

She stared up into his face. He looked kind and understanding and at the same time detached.

She said, 'You're going to be married.'

He nodded, smiling a little. 'Yes, and very soon. Goodnight, Serena.'

He had gone. She stood looking at the door and seething with temper nicely mixed with such a deep sorrow she didn't dare think about it.

'He was laughing!' she told Beauty in a furious voice. 'Not so that you could see, but inside him.' She flung a cushion at the door to relieve her feelings, then burst into tears. 'I dare say he's been wanting to get rid of me for weeks—he put the words into my mouth, didn't he?' she asked wildly. 'So that he didn't have to sack me.'

She sat there grizzling and muttering, not at all her usual quiet self, clasping a mildly protesting Beauty to her, her head in such a tangle of misery that she had no idea what she was saying. A good thing too, for her remarks, uttered in a tear-sodden voice, had become hopelessly illogical.

She went to bed finally and lay awake until after five o'clock, when she dropped off into an exhausted sleep and didn't wake until Beauty, wanting her breakfast, woke her. She got up then, fed the little cat and put the kettle on. A cup of tea would be welcome; she had a headache, and one glance in the looking-glass had sent her spirits back into the soles of her feet. 'I wonder what he's doing now?' she asked Beauty as she sipped very strong tea.

Marc was at his desk. He had just made three very satisfactory phone calls, and all that remained now was to go and see Mrs Bishop. He had already had a talk with Bishop while he breakfasted. He got up, whistling, and with Harley at his heels took himself off for a walk in Hyde Park.

Serena squeezed under the shower, washed her hair, did her nails and did the best she could with her face; never a beauty, she had suffered from her weeping. Then she dressed, had a cup of coffee and took herself out for a brisk walk. She went in the opposite direction to the hospital through the shabby streets for the most part quiet after the previous evening's junketing, and as she went she did her best to discard all thoughts save those appertaining to her future. There were three days left of the week, precious little time in which to decide what to do next. It would be best if she delayed giving Mrs Peck a week's notice until she had somewhere to go. She hesitated to ask Aunt Edith if she might stay with them until she had found a job, since there was no knowing how long that might take. She had a little money, enough to tide her over for a week or so; she would be able to keep her room on for another week and then pay a week in lieu of notice if something turned up. Tomorrow, she told herself firmly, she would go to the public library and scan the jobs columns in the national newspapers. There were the nursing magazines too, and *The Lady*. The least Marc could do would be to give her a good reference. She turned for home, pondering where she would like to live; somewhere in the West Country, or failing that the Cotswolds. Far enough away from London to be able to start a new life...

When she got back to her room there was the rest of the day to get through, and that, if possible, without thinking about Marc. An impossibility.

She dreaded seeing him the next morning. She got to the hospital early, typed out her resignation, and since there was a clinic later she was able to nip down to OPD, and put the envelope on his desk. That done, she felt better, or at least resigned, and, since there was work waiting for her on her desk, she went ahead with it until it was time to go to the clinic.

As usual after a holiday, the waiting-hall bulged with patients, and for once Serena was pleased, for that meant she wouldn't have a moment for anything but work all day. Marc was already there as she went in, but so were all the others—his registrar, sister and three students—so it was easy to address a general good morning without looking at him.

The clinic, once started, went on and on. Someone brought them coffee, but it grew cold before they could spare time to drink it, and the doctor went steadily ahead, giving his attention to each patient in

turn, seemingly tireless, and when the last patient had
gone he left at once to do a delayed ward round, but
not without thanking his companions for their
morning's work.

'Thank heavens that's over,' said Sister, sweeping
up notes and charts and X-ray forms. 'I'm famished!
That man's a workaholic. A good thing he's getting
married—it'll give him something else to think about.'

Everyone had gone but Serena, who found it
necessary to make some sort of a reply. 'Will you go
to the wedding?' was all she could think of to say.

'I believe it's to be a quiet affair, but, knowing him,
he'll invite those who work for him. He may be a
baron in his own country and a noted consultant in
this one and as rich as Croesus, so I've heard, but
he's no snob, and so very kind.' She paused. 'He'd
be angry if I told you some of the things he's done
to help out, and never a breath of what he's done for
anyone.' Sister sighed. 'Ah, well, his wife's a lucky
woman. Let's go to the canteen and see what's left.'

For the rest of that week Serena hardly set eyes on
Marc. Work appeared on her desk—reams of it, for
all the world as though he intended to get the last
ounce of work out of her before she left. In a way,
she was glad of it, for she was too busy to brood. By
the time she got home each evening and fed Beauty,
got her own supper and studied the vacancies in the
various magazines and newspapers she had bought on
the way, she found that there was little time to do
more than go to bed.

She was miserably unhappy, but to get her future
settled had priority over personal feelings, and so far
there had been nothing she had wanted to apply for.
She had decided to try to find a post as receptionist

in a country practice, as far away from London as possible, and failing that a job in one of the smaller provincial hospitals.

The last morning came. There was the usual pile of work waiting for her, but first of all she went along to see Mrs Dunn. She had already told that lady that she was leaving and had been relieved when she had taken it for granted that Serena wanted to be nearer her mother now that she had remarried. Indeed, most of the people she knew in the hospital thought the same thing, and she didn't enlighten them; it made her leaving easier.

There was an afternoon clinic, and she took care to be in OPD before Marc should arrive so that she could bid everyone there goodbye before he got there. In that way she would be able to slip away at the end of the clinic, type up the notes and then leave quickly and quietly.

There weren't as many patients as usual, and it was barely four o'clock when the doctor got up from his desk. He said his usual thanks to everyone there, and then turned to Serena.

'I'm sure that we all wish you a very happy future, Serena. We shall miss you. I hope you find exactly what you have in mind and that, when you have, you will send us a postcard.' He smiled nicely at her, nodded briskly and went away.

'Now that was a funny thing to say,' said Sister, 'And he didn't shake hands or anything...'

'Well, I dare say I shall see him again before I go, Sister. I've got these notes to type for him.'

A remark which satisfied Sister, although there was no truth in it. She had seen Marc for the last time...

The notes didn't take long. Serena put them in their folder ready to hand to the head porter as she left, tidied her desk for the last time, went to wish Mrs Dunn and the other typists goodbye, got into her outdoor things and left the office. She had the strange feeling that it wasn't really happening, that on Monday she would be there again, just as usual, that none of this was happening to her.

However, it was. She went down to the front entrance, handed in the folders and walked to the door. She was almost there when the porter called after her. 'Miss Proudfoot, you're wanted in Matron's office. Would you go there now, please?'

Serena turned round, searching her head to think what it was that she had omitted to do before she left. Surely Matron didn't expect her to say a personal goodbye to her? She hardly knew her, only as a formidable figure whom she had occasionally encountered in the hospital corridors.

She paused by the lodge. 'Have I done something?' she asked. 'Didn't Matron say why she wanted me?'

'No, Miss Proudfoot, just the message.'

'I suppose I'd better go?'

'I would if I were you, love,' said the head porter, all at once quite fatherly.

She went down the main corridor and knocked on Matron's office door, and when the green light above it showed, opened the door and went in.

Matron wasn't there, but Marc was, sitting on the side of the desk, studying his shoes.

Serena stood staring at him, going slowly pale. 'Oh, no—not you,' she muttered, and turned tail, to be halted by his placid,

'Don't run away, Serena.' He got off the desk and came slowly towards her, stretched out an arm and closed the door, then put the arm round her. 'I always thought,' he observed thoughtfully, 'that a girl knew when a man was in love with her.'

She gave a wriggle to escape his arm, and he put the other one around her as well and clamped her gently against his great chest. She said in a small voice muffled by his waistcoat, 'You're going to get married...everyone says so—so did you.'

'Well, of course I am. To you, my dearest love.'

'But you gave me the sack!' She sniffed dolefully. 'You didn't mind a bit...'

'Of course I didn't. I was delighted. You're no longer working for me, we can marry as soon as I can arrange a licence.'

She sniffed and lifted her head. 'You haven't asked me if I want to marry you.'

He kissed her gently. 'Will you marry me, my darling? But only if you want to.'

'Of course I want to,' said Serena tartly, and then in a loving little voice, 'Oh, Marc, I've been so unhappy!'

'Not any more, my love. I'll make sure of that.' He kissed her again, this time at some length. 'Now we will go home and fix a date for the wedding.'

'You mean to Park Street?'

'Heaven forbid!' He ran a gentle finger down her cheek. 'You're not going back there.'

'I must—Beauty and all my things...'

'Beauty is in the car outside, I fetched her half an hour ago, and Mrs Peck packed what she thought you might need—you're coming back with me, dearest.'

Serena, wrapped in a mist of happiness, made one more effort to be sensible. 'Mother—and Aunt Edith, and your family...'

'We will send a telex to your mother. As for Aunt Edith, I phoned her yesterday. You're to stay there until your uncle marries us. My mother and the family know too, they can't wait to welcome you.'

'You were very sure.'

'Oh, yes—that I loved you and would marry you.'

'I might have said no,' said Serena, making a great effort to assert herself.

'But you said yes, my darling.' His voice was gentle and loving.

She nodded into his shoulder. 'You're quite sure?' she asked anxiously.

He didn't reply, but kissed her again instead; a most satisfactory answer, blotting out any doubts there might still be at the back of her head. 'And now we will go home,' he told her, which was exactly what she most wanted to do.

HARLEQUIN
Romance

A Christmas tradition...

Imagine spending Christmas in New
Orleans with a blind stranger and his aged
guide dog—when you're supposed to be
there on your honeymoon!
#3163 Every Kind of Heaven
by Bethany Campbell

Imagine spending Christmas with a man
you once "married"—in a mock ceremony
at the age of eight!
#3166 The Forgetful Bride
by Debbie Macomber

*Available in December 1991, wherever
Harlequin books are sold.*

RXM